THE ASSASSINATOR'S GAME

BY

Nicholas Armstorng Jr

MAPLE
PUBLISHERS

THE ASSASSINATOR'S GAME

Author: Nicholas Armstorng Jr

Copyright © 2025 Nicholas Armstrong Jr

First Published in 2025

ISBN 978-1-83538-677-4 (Paperback)
     978-1-83538-678-1 (Hardback)
     978-1-83538-679-8 (E-Book)

Book cover design and Book layout by:
     White Magic Studios
     www.whitemagicstudios.co.uk

Published by:
     Maple Publishers
     Fairbourne Drive, Atterbury,
     Milton Keynes,
     MK10 9RG, UK
     www.maplepublishers.com

A CIP catalogue record for this title is available from the British Library.

1

THE ASSASSINATION OF PETER ERICKSON

Once upon a time there lived a man. There lived a great man. There lived a good man. There lived a strong man. There lived a police man. There lived a great police man. There lived a good police man. There lived a police man in New York. There lived a police man called Peter Erickson. And that police man was me. There lived a police officer. There lived a police officer in New York. I was against the death penalty. I was against the death penalty in America. I was against the American justice system. I wanted to change the American justice system. I wrote the book of justice. I took the book of justice. I grabbed my machine gun. I grabbed my black machine gun. I placed the machine gun. I placed it inside my pocket. I walked outside my house. I grabbed my motorbike. I grabbed a black motorbike. I sat on the motorbike. I sat on a black motorbike. I reached my hands forward. I grabbed the motorbike. I pushed my feet downwards. I sparked my motorbike. I sparked it the first time. I sparked it the second time. I sparked it the third time. I saw something. I saw my motorbike. I saw it running. I saw it running faster. I rode on my motorbike. I rode with my head downwards. I rode faster. I rode like a police officer. I rode faster. I rode past police cars. I rode faster. I rode past police stations. I rode faster. I rode past New York police stations. I rode faster. I rode past New York police cars. I rode faster. I rode past train stations. I rode faster. I rode past New York train stations. I rode faster. I rode farther. I rode past New York. I rode faster. I rode inside California. I rode faster. I rode past California police cars. I rode faster. I rode past California police stations. I rode faster. I rode past California train stations. I rode faster. I rode past California Mountains. I rode farther. I turned around. I saw a man. I saw a white man. I saw a man wearing a black jacket. I saw a white man wearing a black jacket. I saw him sitting on a motorbike. I saw him sitting on a black motorbike. I saw him riding. I saw him riding on his motorbike. I saw him riding faster. I saw him following me. I saw him riding faster. I saw him chasing me. I turned around. I sparked my motorbike. I sparked it the second time. I sparked it the third time. I saw something. I saw something happening. I saw my motorbike. I saw it running. I saw it running faster. I rode faster. I rode on my running motorbike. I rode with my head downwards. I rode in California. I rode faster. I turned around. I saw the white man. I saw him riding. I saw him riding faster. I saw him chasing me. I saw him getting closer. I saw him getting closer to me. I turned around. I reached my hand inside my pocket. I grabbed my machine gun. I pulled out my black machine gun. I turned around. I pointed my machine gun. I pointed it at the white man. I shot the white man. I shot him the first time. I shot him the second time. I shot him the third time. I saw the white man. I saw nothing. I saw nothing happening. I saw nothing. I saw nothing happening to him. I saw the white man. I saw a strong man. I saw him strong. I pointed my machine gun at him again. I shot the white man. I shot him again. I shot him the first time. I shot him the second time. I shot him the third time. I saw nothing. I saw nothing happening. I saw nothing. I saw nothing happening to the white man. I saw nothing happening to him. I saw the white man. I saw him strong. I saw him strong again. I looked at the white man. I saw the white man. I saw him riding on his motorbike. I saw him riding faster. I saw him chasing me. I saw the white man. I saw him riding faster. I saw him getting closer. I saw him getting closer to me. I saw the white man. I saw him putting his hand inside his pocket. I saw him pulling out something. I saw him pulling out something strange. I saw him pulling out a machine gun. I saw him pulling out a black machine gun. I saw the white man. I saw him holding his machine gun. I saw him holding a black machine gun. I saw him pointing his machine gun. I saw him pointing his black machine gun. I saw him pointing it forward. I saw him pointing it at me. I saw the white man. I saw him shooting. I saw him shooting me. I saw him shooting me the first time. I saw him shooting me the second time. I saw him shooting me the third time. I saw something. I saw something happening. I saw something. I saw something happening to me. I saw something. I saw something happening. I saw something. I saw something strange. I saw something. I saw something strange happening. I saw something. I saw something strange happening to me. I saw me flying. I saw myself lying on my motorbike. I saw me flying from my motorbike. I saw me dropping. I dropped on the ground. I dropped on a road. I dropped on a lonely road. I dropped on a road in California. I was breathless. I was weakened. I was in weakness. I suffered in pain. I was not shaking. I was not moving. I was dying. I was lying on the ground. I was lying on a road. I was lying on a lonely road. I was lying on a road in California. I grabbed my chest. I saw something. I saw something strange. I saw blood. I saw blood flowing. I saw blood running from my chest. I was bleeding. I saw blood on my chest. I saw blood on the ground. I was breathless. I was not breathing. I saw a static for a major. I was motionless. I was not shaking. I was not moving. I was dying. I saw the white man. I saw him parking. I saw him parking his motorbike. I saw him parking it in front of me. I saw him walking. I saw him walking forward. I saw him walking towards me. I saw him in front of me. I saw him looking at me. I was dead. I saw someone. I saw the white man. I saw someone. I saw a police officer. I saw my fellow police officer. I saw Snogun. I saw him turning around. I saw him looking around. I saw him looking for something. I saw him looking for the book of justice. I saw Snogun. I saw the police man. I saw the police man from New York. I saw the white police man. I saw the police officer. I saw my fellow police officer. I saw Snogun. I saw him searching the book of justice. I saw him discovering the book of justice. I saw Snogun. I saw him holding the book of justice. I saw him turning around. I saw him walking. I saw him walking forward. I saw him walking towards Peter Erickson. I saw him walking towards the New York police officer. I saw him walking towards me. I saw Snogun. I saw him in front of me. I saw him holding the book of justice. I saw him holding my book of justice. I saw him looking at me. I saw him smiling. I saw him smiling at Peter Erickson. I saw him smiling at the white police officer. I I saw him smiling at me. I saw Snogun. I saw him turning around. I saw him walking. I saw him walking forward. I saw him walking towards his motorbike. I saw him in front of his motorbike. I saw him looking at his motorbike. I saw him looking at his black motorbike. I saw him holding the book of justice. I saw Snogun. I saw him jumping on his motorbike. I saw him sitting on his motorbike. I saw him reaching his hand downwards. I saw him placing the book of justice. I saw him putting it inside his pocket. I saw him reaching his hands forward. I saw him grabbing his motorbike. I saw him pushing his feet downwards. I saw him pushing harder. I saw him sparking. I saw him sparking his motorbike. I saw something. I saw something happening. I saw his motorbike. I saw it running. I saw it running faster. I saw Snogun. I saw him riding. I saw him riding on his motorbike. I saw him riding with his head downwards. I saw him riding past Peter Erickson. I saw him riding. I saw him riding faster. I saw him riding past a dead police officer. I saw him riding faster. I saw him riding past a dead New York police officer. I saw him riding faster. I saw him riding past me. I saw Snogun. I saw him riding. I saw him riding faster. I saw him riding in California. I saw him riding faster. I saw him riding past California Mountains. I saw him riding farther. I saw Snogun. I saw him approaching somewhere. I saw him approaching a mansion. I saw him approaching a governor's mansion. I saw him approaching the mansion of a governor. I saw Snogun. I saw him in front of a mansion. I saw him in front of the governor's mansion. I saw Snogun. I saw him parking. I saw him parking his motorbike. I saw him jumping off his motorbike. I saw him standing in front of the governor's mansion. I saw him looking at a white mansion. I saw him looking at the governor's mansion. I saw him walking. I saw him walking forward. I saw him in front of a giant gate. I looked at the giant gate. I saw something. I saw something strange. I saw something. I saw something strange happening. I saw the governor's gate. I saw the gate opening. I saw the gate opened. I saw the gate opening faster. I saw Snogun. I saw him walking. I saw him walking inside the gate. I saw Snogun. I saw him inside the governor's mansion. I saw the gate. I saw the gate closing. I saw the gate closing faster. I saw Snogun. I saw him inside the governor's mansion. I saw him climbing. I saw him climbing upwards. I saw Snogun. I saw him upwards. I saw him in front of a white door. I saw Snogun. I saw him opening the door. I saw him inside an office. I saw him inside the governor's office. I saw Snogun. I saw him in front of the governor. I saw him looking at the governor. I saw Snogun. I saw him reaching his hand downwards. I saw him putting his hand inside his pocket. I saw him pulling out his gun. I saw him pulling out his machine gun. I saw Snogun. I saw him pointing his gun. I saw him pointing his machine gun. I saw him pointing it at the governor. I saw him shooting. I saw him shooting the governor. I saw him shooting the governor the first time. I saw him shooting the governor the second time. I saw him shooting the governor the third time. I saw him shooting the governor multiple times. I saw the governor. I saw him dying. I saw him dead. I saw him murdered. I saw him brutally murdered. I saw him sitting on his chair. I saw blood on his chest. I saw blood running. I saw blood running on his chest. I saw the governor. I saw the governor of California. I saw him bleeding. I saw him dying. I saw him dead. I saw Snogun. I saw him walking. I saw him walking towards a wardrobe. I saw him in front of the wardrobe. I saw him opening the wardrobe. I saw him entering the wardrobe. I saw him inside the wardrobe. I saw him looking at shirts. I saw him looking at trousers. I saw him looking at shoes. I saw him looking at coats. I saw Snogun. I saw him removing a shirt. I saw him wearing the shirt. I saw him removing a trouser. I saw him wearing the trouser. I saw him removing a coat. I saw him wearing the coat. I saw him removing a shoe. I saw him wearing the shoe. I saw Snogun. I saw him turning around. I saw him walking. I saw him walking outside the wardrobe. I saw him outside the wardrobe. I saw him looking at the governor. I saw him looking at the dead governor. I looked at the governor. I saw the governor. I saw something. I saw something strange. I saw something. I saw something strange happening. I saw the governor. I saw the governor of California. I saw the dead governor. I saw him vanishing. I saw him vanished. I saw him no more. I saw Snogun. I saw him walking. I saw him walking forward. I saw him walking towards a table. I saw him in front of the governor's table. I saw him reaching his hand downwards. I saw him putting his hand inside his pocket. I saw him pulling out something. I saw him pulling out the book of justice. I saw Snogun. I saw him holding the book of justice. I saw him holding my book of justice. I saw him placing it on the governor's table. I saw him walking round the table. I saw him sitting on a chair. I saw him sitting on the governor's chair. I saw Snogun. I saw him becoming a governor. I saw Snogun. I saw the governor of California. I saw Snogun. I saw him opening the book of justice. I saw him looking inside the book of justice. I saw Snogun. I saw him not happy. I saw him not happy about a change. I saw him not happy for a change in the American justice system. I saw him happy about the death penalty. I saw him happy for a death sentence. I saw him happy for death sentences. I saw him happy to maintain the death penalty in America. I saw Snogun. I saw him not ready. I saw him not ready for a change. I saw him not ready for a change in the American justice system. I saw Snogun. I saw the governor of California. I saw him ready. I saw him happy for executions. I saw him ready for executions. I saw him ready for the executions of American prisoners. I was lying on the ground. I was lying on a road. I was lying on a lonely road. I was lying dead. I was dead on the ground. I was dead on the road. I was dead on a lonely road. I saw someone. I saw a black man. I saw him riding on his motorbike. I saw him riding. I saw him riding in California. I saw him riding farther. I saw him approaching Peter Erickson. I saw him approaching the New York police officer. I saw him approaching a dead police officer. I saw him approaching me. I saw a black man. I saw him sitting on his motorbike. I saw him wearing a black jacket. I saw him in front of me. I saw him parking. I saw him parking his motorbike. I saw him parking in front of me. I saw him jumping off his motorbike. I saw him walking. I saw him walking forward. I saw him walking towards me. I saw the black man. I saw him in front of me. I saw him looking at me. I saw him looking at a dead police officer. I saw the black man. I saw him grabbing me. I saw him grabbing me. I saw him holding me to the ground. I saw him helping. I saw him helping me. I saw him supporting me. I saw him looking at me. I saw him looking in my eyes. I saw him looking in my blue eyes. I saw him seeing me dead. I saw the black man. I saw him sad. I saw him upset. I saw him worried. I saw the black man. I saw him turning around. I saw him looking around. I looked farther. I saw hundreds of police cars. I saw hundreds of police cars coming. I saw hundreds of police cars. I saw hundreds of California police cars. I saw hundreds of California police cars coming. I saw the black man. I saw him looking around. I saw him looking around him. I saw him looking at police cars. I saw him looking at hundreds of police cars. I looked around. I looked around at the black man. I looked around me. I saw hundreds of police officers. I saw them surrounding the black man. I saw them surrounding me. I saw them speaking. I saw them speaking to the black man. I saw them speaking. I saw them telling him to put his hands up. I saw them telling him to give up. I saw the California police officers. I saw them rushing forward. I saw them arresting the black man. I saw them putting him inside a police van. I saw the California police officers. I saw them driving their police cars. I saw them taking the black man. I saw them taking him farther. I saw them taking him to a notorious California prison. I saw them taking him farther. I saw them taking him to Texas. I saw them taking his farther. I saw them taking him to a prison outside California. I saw them taking him to Texas prison. I saw the black man. I saw him coming out the police van. I saw police officers. I saw them grabbing the black man. I saw them grabbing his hands. I saw them taking him inside a notorious prison. I saw them putting him inside a cell. I saw the California police officers. I saw them saying goodbye. I saw them saying goodbye to the black man. I saw them saying goodbye to the Texas prison officers. I saw the prison officers. I saw them giving the black man something. I saw them giving him something to wear. I saw them giving him clothes. I saw them giving him prison clothes. I saw the black man. I saw him wearing his prison clothes. I saw the black man. I saw him in court the following week. I saw the judge. I saw him looking at the black man. I saw him speaking. I saw him speaking to the black man. I saw a white judge. I saw a judge called John Patterson. I saw him asking the black man for his name. I saw the black man. I saw him standing up. I saw him looking at the judge. I saw him speaking. I saw him speaking to the judge. I saw him replying to the judge. I saw him replying that he was called Black Arnold. I saw the judge. I saw him telling him to sit down. I saw Black Arnold. I saw the black man. I saw the black prisoner. I saw him sitting down. I saw the Jury's spokesperson. I saw him speaking. I saw him speaking to the judge. I saw him demanding for a death penalty. I saw him demanding a death penalty for Black Arnold. I saw the Jury's spokesperson. I saw him demanding a death sentence. I saw him demanding a death sentence for Black Arnold. I saw the judge. I saw him accepting his demand for a death penalty. I saw the judge. I saw him looking at black Arnold. I saw him telling the black man to stand up. I saw Black Arnold. I saw the black man. I saw him standing up. I saw him looking at the judge. I saw the judge. I saw him looking at the black man. I saw him looking at Black Arnold. I saw the judge. I saw him sentencing Black Arnold. I saw him sentencing the black man. I saw him sentencing the black prisoner. I saw the judge. I saw him giving a death penalty. I saw him sentencing Black Arnold to death. I saw Black Arnold. I saw the black man. I saw an innocent man. I saw the prisoner. I saw an innocent prisoner. I saw Black Arnold. I saw him sentenced to death. I saw him being taken back to prison. I saw him serving his death sentence. I saw my funeral in New York. I saw my families. I saw my friends and families at my funeral. I saw my families. I saw them mourning. I saw them mourning the death of Peter Erickson. I saw them mourning the death of a New York police officer. I saw my families. I saw them mourning my death. I saw them putting my body inside a coffin. I saw them putting my coffin inside a funeral car. I saw them driving me. I saw them driving me to the cemetery. I saw them driving me to a cemetery in New York. I saw my families. I saw them arriving at the cemetery. I saw them arriving at a cemetery in New York. I saw my families. I saw them coming out the funeral car. I saw them opening the car boot. I saw them carrying my coffin. I saw them burying Peter Erickson. I saw them burying a police officer. I saw them burying a New York police officer. I saw them burying me. I saw my families. I saw them turning around. I saw them leaving the cemetery. I saw them walking. I saw them walking towards the funeral car. I saw them in front of the funeral car. I saw my families. I saw them turning around. I saw them waving. I saw them waving me good bye. I saw them opening the car door. I saw them sitting inside the car. I saw them driving the funeral car. I saw my families. I saw them returning home. I saw them returned back home.

2

THE ASSASSINATION MAN's JOURNEY

FROM

NEW YORK TO FLORIDA

I was buried in New York Cemetery. I was buried in a black graveyard. I saw my families. I saw them returned back home. Once upon a time. I saw someone. I saw someone dead. I saw a dead man. I saw a dead man and that dead man was Peter Erickson. I saw a dead man and that dead man was me. I saw a police man. I saw a dead police man. I saw a dead police man and that dead police man was Peter Erickson. I saw a dead police man. I saw a dead police man and that dead police man was me. I saw a dead police officer. I saw a dead police officer and that dead police officer was Peter Erickson. I saw a dead police officer. I saw a dead police officer and that dead police officer was me. Once upon a time. I saw a buried man. I saw a buried man and that buried man was Peter Erickson. I saw a buried man. I saw a buried man and that buried man was me. I saw a buried police man. I saw a buried police man and that buried police man was Peter Erickson. I saw a buried police man. I saw a buried police man and that buried police man was me. I saw a buried police officer. I saw a buried police officer and that buried police officer was Peter Erickson. I saw a buried police officer. I saw a buried police officer and that buried police officer was me. Once upon a time. I saw a buried New York police man. I saw a buried New York police man and that buried New York police man was Peter Erickson. I saw a buried New York police man. I saw a buried New York police man and that buried New York police man was me. I saw a buried New York police officer. I saw a buried New York police officer and that buried New York police officer was Peter Erickson. I saw a buried New York police officer. I saw a buried New York police officer and that buried New York police officer was me. Once upon a time. Five years after my burial. Years after I was buried. Five years after I was buried. I rose from the dead. I rose in the cemetery. I rose in the graveyard. I rose upwards. I turned into someone. I turned into someone strange. I turned into human. I turned into a human robot. I stood in front of many graves. I walked. I walked forward. I walked past the graveyard. I walked past many graves. I saw many graves. I walked outside the graveyard. I walked outside the New York cemetery. I came across somewhere. I came across somewhere lonely. I came across a road. I came across a lonely road. I stood behind the road. I stood behind a lonely road. I twisted my head around. I looked on the left side of the road. I looked on the right side of the road. I saw riding men. I saw them riding. I saw them riding on their motorbikes. I saw them riding faster. I saw them riding past me. I saw riding women. I saw them riding. I saw them riding on their motorbikes. I saw them riding faster. I saw them riding past me. I saw driving men. I saw them driving. I saw them driving their cars. I saw them driving in their cars. I saw them driving faster. I saw them driving past me. I saw driving women. I saw them driving. I saw them driving their cars. I saw them driving in their cars. I saw them driving faster. I saw them driving past me. I saw police men. I saw them driving. I saw them driving their cars. I saw them driving their police cars. I saw them driving in their police cars. I saw them driving faster. I saw them driving past me. I saw police women. I saw them driving. I saw them driving their police cars. I saw them driving in their police cars. I saw them driving faster. I saw them driving past me. I twisted my head to my right hand side. I looked farther. I saw a police man. I saw a New York police man. I saw him sitting on a motorbike. I saw him sitting on a black and white motorbike. I saw him wearing a police jacket. I saw him riding. I saw him riding on his motorbike. I saw him riding towards me. I saw him riding forward. I saw him riding faster. I saw a police officer. I saw a New York police officer. I saw him in front of me. I saw him parking his motorbike. I saw him looking at me. I saw him speaking. I saw him speaking to me. I saw him asking me for something. I saw him asking me for my name. I walked. I walked forward. I walked towards the police man. I walked towards the police officer. I walked towards him. I stood in front of him. I looked at the police man. I replied to the police man. I looked at the police officer. I replied to the police officer. I replied to him that I am Peter Erickson. I pushed my hand forward. I pushed harder. I grabbed the police man. I grabbed his neck. I raised my hand upwards. I was holding the police man. I was holding him upwards. I was holding him with one hand. I looked at the police man. I looked at him. I rolled my eyes. I rolled my robot eyes. I smiled. I smiled at the police man. I smiled at him. I threw the police man. I threw him forward. I saw the police man. I saw him farther. I saw him flying. I saw him flying backwards. I saw him dropping. I saw him dropped on the ground. I saw him dropped on a lonely ground. I saw him lying on the ground. I saw him lying on a lonely ground. I saw him lying on a road. I saw him lying on a lonely road. I saw him breathless. I saw him not breathing. I saw him suffering. I saw him in heavy pain. I saw a static for a major. I saw him motionless. I saw him not shaking. I saw him not moving. I saw him dying. I saw him dying on a road. I saw him dying on a lonely road. I looked forward. I saw the police man. I saw his motorbike. I walked farther. I walked towards the police man. I walked towards a dying police man. I stood in front of the police man. I stood in front of a dying police man. I searched the police man. I searched a dying police man. I searched for something. I searched for a gun. I looked around. I looked farther. I saw his gun. I saw his machine gun. I saw it farther. I walked farther. I discovered his gun. I discovered his machine gun. I stood in front of his gun. I grabbed his gun. I grabbed his machine gun. I placed his machine gun. I placed it inside my pocket. I turned around. I walked. I walked farther. I walked past the police man. I walked past a dying police man. I walked farther. I walked towards his motorbike. I stood in front of his motorbike. I jumped on his motorbike. I sat on his motorbike. I reached my hands forward. I grabbed the motorbike. I pushed my feet downwards. I sparked the motorbike. I sparked it the first time. I sparked it the second time. I sparked it the third time. I saw something. I saw something happening. I saw the motorbike. I saw it running. I saw it running faster. I rode on the motorbike. I rode on a police motorbike. I rode faster. I rode past a dying police man. I rode farther. I came across somewhere. I came across a police station. I came across a New York police station. I parked my motorbike. I parked it in front of the police station. I jumped off my motorbike. I reached my hand inside my pocket. I pulled out my machine gun. I was holding my machine gun. I walked forward. I walked towards the police station. I stood in front of the police station. I stood in front of the police gates. I saw something. I saw something strange. I saw something. I saw something strange happening. I saw the police gates. I saw it opening. I saw it opened. I walked inside the police station. I saw one police man. I saw him holding his gun. I saw him holding a machine gun. I saw him looking at me. I saw him pointing his machine gun. He pointed his machine gun at me. I saw him running. I saw him running towards me. I saw him shooting. I saw him shooting me. I saw him shooting me the first time. I saw him shooting me the second time. I saw him shooting me the third time. I saw him shooting me multiple times. I saw the police man. I saw him in front of me. I pushed my hand forward. I grabbed the police man. I grabbed his neck. I was holding the police man. I was holding him with one hand. I raised him upwards. I looked at him. I smiled. I smiled at him. I rolled my eyes. I rolled my robot eyes. I rolled my blue eyes. I threw the police man. I threw him inside the police station. I threw him farther. I saw the police man. I saw him flying. I saw him flying farther. I saw him dropping. I saw him dropped on the ground. I saw him dropped on a black ground. I saw the police man. I saw a dying man. I saw him lying on the ground. I saw him lying on a black ground. I saw him suffering. I saw him in pain. I saw him in heavy pain. I saw him dying. I saw him breathless. I saw him motionless. I saw him not shaking. I saw him not moving. I walked farther. I walked towards the police man. I walked towards a dying man. I stood in front of him. I looked at him. I pulled out my machine gun. I shot the police man. I shot a dying man. I shot him the first time. I shot him the second time. I shot him the third time. I shot him multiple times. I assassinated a police man. I assassinated a New York police man. I assassinated a dying police man. I looked farther. I saw a lot of police men. I saw them inside the police station. I saw them inside New York police station. I saw them farther. I saw them running. I saw them running towards me. I saw them pulling out their machine guns. I saw them shooting. I saw them shooting me. I saw them shooting me the first time. I saw them shooting me the second time. I saw them shooting me the third time. I saw them shooting me multiple times. I saw nothing. I saw nothing happening. I saw nothing. I saw nothing happening to me. Nothing happened. Nothing happened to me. I pulled out my machine gun. I pointed it at the police officers. I pointed it at shooting police officers. I pointed it farther. I walked forward. I walked towards the police men. I walked towards shooting police officers. I shot the police officers. I shot the police officers the first time. I shot the police officers the second time. I shot the police officers the third time. I shot the police officers multiple times. I assassinated New York police officers. I assassinated them with one shot. I assassinated them with two shots. I assassinated them with triple shots. I assassinated them with multiple shots. I saw the New York police officers. I saw them assassinated. I saw them dropping. I saw them dropped on the ground. I saw them lying on the ground. I saw them dying. I saw them dying on the ground. I saw the police officers. I saw them dead. I saw them dead inside a police station. I saw them dead inside a New York police station. I walked inside the New York police station. I shot all the police officers. I shot them one time. I shot them two times. I shot them three times. I shot them multiple times. I saw the New York police officers. I saw them dropping. I saw them dropped on the ground. I saw them dying. I saw them dying on the ground. I saw them breathless. I saw them not breathing. I saw them weakened. I saw them in weakness. I saw them suffering. I saw them in heavy pain. I saw them motionless. I saw them not shaking. I saw them not moving. I saw them lifeless. I saw them dead. I turned around. I walked outside the New York police station. I walked forward. I walked towards my motorbike. I stood in front of my motorbike. I jumped on my motorbike. I sat on my motorbike. I reached my hand downwards. I opened my pocket. I placed my machine gun. I placed it inside my pocket. I reached my hands forward. I grabbed my motorbike. I pushed my feet downwards. I sparked my motorbike. I sparked it the first time. I sparked it the second time. I sparked it the third time. I sparked it multiple times. I saw something. I saw something happening. I saw my motorbike. I saw it running. I saw it running faster. I rode on my motorbike. I rode with my head downwards. I rode faster. I rode past the New York police station. I rode faster. I rode past motorbike riders. I rode faster. I turned around. I saw a lot of police cars. I saw a lot of police cars chasing me. I saw a lot of police motorbikes. I saw a lot of police motorbikes chasing me. I saw police officers. I saw New York police officers. I saw them inside their police cars. I saw them driving their police cars. I saw them chasing me. I saw them pulling out their machine guns. I saw them shooting. I saw them shooting me. I saw them shooting me from their car window. I saw a lot of police officers. I saw New York police officers. I saw them riding on their motorbikes. I saw them chasing me. I saw them pulling out their machine guns. I saw them pointing their machine guns. I saw them pointing their guns at me. I saw them shooting. I saw them shooting me. I saw nothing. I saw nothing happening to me. Nothing happened. Nothing happened to me. I grabbed my machine gun. I pointed it at the police cars. I shot the police cars. I saw the police cars. I saw them bombing. I saw them bombed. I saw the police cars. I saw them on fire. I saw them burning. I saw them burned. I pointed my machine gun. I pointed it at police officers. I pointed it at police officers riding on motorbikes. I shot the police officers. I shot them the first time. I shot them the second time. I shot them the third time. I shot them multiple times. I saw the police officers. I saw them flying. I saw them flying on their motorbikes. I saw them dropping. I saw them dropped on the road. I saw their motorbikes. I saw their motorbikes bombing. I saw their motorbikes. I saw it bombing. I saw it bombed. I saw it on fire. I saw it burning. I turned around. I placed my machine gun. I placed it inside my pocket. I pushed my hands forward. I grabbed my motorbike. I rode on my motorbike. I rode with my head downwards. I rode faster. I rode past the New York police officers. I rode past dead police officers. I rode past their motorbikes. I rode past their burning motorbikes. I rode farther. I came across a prison. I came across a New York prison. I parked my motorbike. I parked it in front of the prison. I put my hand inside my pocket. I pulled out my machine gun. I walked. I walked forward. I walked towards the prison. I stood in front of the prison. I stood in front a gate. I stood in front a giant gate. I looked at the gate. I rolled my eyes. I rolled my robot eyes. I rolled my blue eyes. I saw something. I saw something strange. I saw something. I saw something strange happening. I saw the prison gate. I saw the gate opening. I saw it opened. I walked inside the prison. I shot one prison officer. I walked farther. I opened one door. I walked inside. I saw one prison officer. I saw him sitting on a chair. I saw him wearing a shirt. I pointed my machine gun at him. I shot him. I shot him the first time. I shot him the second time. I shot him multiple times. I shot him dead. I saw the prison officer. I saw him dying. I saw him dead. I saw things scattered around the room. I looked around the room. I saw some keys. I saw black keys. I saw keys for the prison cells. I saw the cells keys. I saw them on the top of the table. I grabbed the cell keys. I walked outside the room. I stood in front of the door. I saw the door. I saw it closing. I saw it closed. I looked farther. I saw a lot of prison officers. I saw them running. I saw them running towards me. I saw them running. I saw them pointing their machine guns. I saw them pointing their machine guns at me. I saw them shooting. I saw them shooting me. I saw them shooting me multiple times. I saw nothing. I saw nothing happening. I saw nothing happening to me. Nothing happened. Nothing happened to me. I pulled out my machine gun. I shot one prison officer. I saw him dropping. I saw him dropped on the ground. I saw him dying. I saw him dead. I shot another prison officer. I saw him dropping. I saw him dropped on the ground. I saw him dying. I saw him dead. I shot all the prison officers. I saw all the prison officers. I saw them dropping. I saw them dropping on the ground. I saw them dropped. I saw them dropped on the ground. I saw them dying. I saw them dead. I assassinated all the prison officers. I saw all the New York prison officers. I saw them assassinated. I saw them assassinated by Peter Erickson. I saw them assassinated by a human robot. I saw them assassinated by me. I walked towards the prison cells. I placed my hand inside my pocket. I pulled out the cells' keys. I walked towards the first cell. I opened the cell. I saw three prisoners. I saw them sleeping. I saw them sleeping on a giant bed. I woke them all up. I freed them. I gave them freedom. I told them to walk outside the prison. I told them to wait outside the prison. I told them to wait for me. I opened all the prison cells. I freed all the prisoners. I gave all of them freedom. I spoke to all the

New York prisoners. I told all of them to walk outside the prison. I told all of them to wait outside the prison. I told all the prisoners to wait for me. I walked farther. I walked outside the New York prison. I saw hundreds of prisoners. I saw them outside the prison. I saw them waiting for me. I walked forward. I walked towards the prisoners. I rolled my eyes. I rolled my robot eyes. I rolled my blue eyes. I saw something. I saw something strange. I saw something. I saw something strange happening. I saw hundreds of motorbikes. I saw them appearing. I saw the appearance of hundred motorbikes. I saw hundreds of motorbikes. I saw them in front of the prisoners. I saw the prisoners. I saw them looking at me. I saw them speaking. I saw them speaking to me. I saw them thanking. I saw them thanking me. I saw the prisoners. I saw the New York prisoners. I saw their head downwards. I saw them saluting me. I saw them speaking. I saw them speaking to me. I saw them saying goodbye. I saw them saying goodbye to me. I saw the New York prisoners. I saw them turning around. I saw them looking at the motorbikes. I saw them walking. I saw them walking forward. I saw them walking towards the motorbikes. I saw them in front of the motorbikes. I saw them jumping on the motorbikes. I saw them sitting on the motorbikes. I saw them grabbing their motorbikes. I saw them pushing their feet downwards. I saw them pushing harder. I saw them sparking their motorbikes. I saw them sparking it the first time. I saw them sparking it the second time. I saw them sparking it the third time. I saw them sparking it multiple times. I saw their motorbikes. I saw their motorbikes running. I saw the New York prisoners. I saw them riding their motorbikes. I saw them riding past me. I saw them riding past the New York prison. I saw them riding farther. I saw them riding back home. I walked towards my motorbike. I jumped on my motorbike. I sat on my motorbike. I opened my pocket. I placed my machine gun. I placed it inside my pocket. I grabbed my motorbike. I pushed my feet downwards. I pushed harder. I sparked my motorbike. I sparked it the first time. I sparked it the second time. I sparked it the third time. I saw something. I saw something happening. I saw my motorbike running. I rode on my motorbike. I rode with my head downwards. I rode faster. I rode past the New York Prison. I rode faster. I rode past police cars. I rode past police motorbikes. I rode past train stations. I rode faster. I rode under bridges. I rode faster. I rode past New York. I rode farther. I came across somewhere. I came across another state. I came across another East coast state. I came across Florida.

3

THE ASSASSINATION MAN's JOURNEY

FROM

FLORIDA TO GEORGIA

I rode on my motorbike. I rode in Florida. I rode with my head downwards. I rode faster. I rode past police cars. I rode faster. I rode past police motorbikes. I rode faster. I rode past driving men. I rode faster. I rode past men driving cars. I rode faster. I rode past riding men. I rode faster. I rode past men riding on motorbikes. I rode faster. I rode past driving women. I rode faster. I rode past women driving cars. I rode faster. I rode past riding women. I rode faster. I rode past women riding on motorbikes. I rode faster. I rode past driving police men. I rode faster. I rode past police men driving police cars. I rode faster. I rode past riding police men. I rode faster. I rode past police men riding on motorbikes. I rode faster. I rode past driving police women. I rode faster. I rode past police women driving police cars. I rode faster. I rode past riding police women. I rode faster. I rode past police women riding on police motorbikes. I rode farther. I came across a police station. I came across Florida police station. I parked my police motorbike. I parked it in front of the police station. I grabbed my machine gun. I jumped off my motorbike. I walked forward. I walked towards the police station. I stood in front of the police station. I stood in front of a gate. I stood in front of a giant gate. I stood in front of a locked gate. I looked at the giant gate. I rolled my eyes. I rolled my blue eyes. I saw something. I saw something happening. I saw something. I saw something strange. I saw something. I saw something strange happening. I saw the police gate. I saw the giant gate. I saw it opening. I saw it opened. I walked. I walked forward. I walked inside the giant gate. I walked inside the police station. I walked inside Florida police station. I entered the police station. I saw myself inside the police station. I saw the gate. I saw the giant gate. I saw it closing. I saw it closing faster. I saw it closed. I saw myself inside the police station. I walked forward. I saw one police officer. I saw him sitting on a police chair. I pulled out my machine gun. I pointed it at the police officer. I shot the police officer. I shot him. I shot him the first time. I shot him the second time. I shot him the third time. I shot him the fourth time. I shot him the fifth time. I shot him the six times. I saw the police officer. I saw nothing. I saw nothing happening. I saw nothing. I saw nothing happening to the police officer. I saw the police officer. I saw nothing happening to him. Nothing happened to the police officer. Nothing happened to him. I saw the police officer. I saw him grabbing his gun. I saw him standing up. I saw him holding his gun. I saw him holding a giant gun. I saw him holding a machine gun. I saw him holding a black machine gun. I saw him looking at me. I saw him pointing his gun. I saw him pointing it at me. I saw him walking. I saw him walking forward. I saw him walking towards me. I saw him walking and shooting. I saw him shooting me. I saw him shooting me one time. I saw him shooting me two times. I saw him shooting me three times. I saw nothing. I saw nothing happening. I saw nothing. I saw nothing happening to me. I saw the police officer. I saw him in front of me. I saw him looking at me. I looked at the police officer. I rolled my eyes. I rolled my blue eyes. I pushed my hand forward. I grabbed the police officer. I grabbed him with one hand. I was holding the police officer. I was holding him with one hand. I raised the police officer. I raised him upwards. I raised him above the sky. I raised him with one hand. I looked at the police officer. I was smiling. I was smiling at him. I smiled. I smiled at him. I rolled my eyes. I rolled my blue eyes. I threw the police officer. I threw him forward. I saw the police officer. I saw him flying. I saw him flying backwards. I saw him flying farther. I saw him dropping. I saw him dropped on the ground. I saw him breathless. I saw him not breathing. I saw him suffering. I saw him in heavy pain. I saw him weakened. I saw him in weakness. I saw him motionless. I saw him not shaking. I saw him not moving. I walked. I walked forward. I walked towards the police man. I walked farther. I saw the police man. I saw the police officer. I saw him lying on the ground. I saw him bleeding. I saw his blood on the ground. I saw him breathless. I saw him not breathing. I saw him motionless. I saw him not shaking. I saw him not moving. I stood in front of the police man. I pulled out my machine gun. I shot the police man. I shot the Florida police man. I shot the Florida police officer. I shot him one time. I shot him two times. I shot him three times. I shot him multiple times. I saw the police man. I saw the police officer. I saw him lying on the ground. I saw him bleeding. I saw him bleeding on the ground. I saw his blood on the ground. I saw him dying. I saw him dying on the ground. I saw him lifeless. I saw him lifeless on the ground. I saw him dead. I saw him dead on the ground. I walked forward. I looked farther. I saw a lot of police officers. I saw a lot of police men. I saw a lot of police women. I saw them farther. I saw them running. I saw them running towards me. I saw them shooting. I saw them running and shooting. I saw them shooting me. I saw them shooting me one time. I saw them shooting me two times. I saw them shooting me three times. I saw them shooting me four times. I saw them shooting me five times. I saw them shooting me six times. I saw them shooting me multiple times. I saw nothing. I saw nothing happening. I saw nothing. I saw nothing happening to me. Nothing happened. Nothing happened to me. I pulled out my machine gun. I pointed it at the police officers. I shot some of the police officers. I shot them one time. I shot them two times. I shot them three times. I shot them multiple times. I shot the police officers. I saw them dropping. I saw them dropped on the ground. I saw them bleeding. I saw their blood on the ground. I saw them dying. I saw them dead. I saw them dead on the ground. I walked. I walked forward. I pushed my hands forward. I pushed harder. I grabbed the police officers. I grabbed two police officers. I grabbed them with two hands. I grabbed them with my two hands. I was holding the two police officers. I was holding them with my two hands. I raised the two police officers. I raised them upwards. I raised them above the sky. I looked at the two police officers. I smiled. I smiled at the two police officers. I rolled my eyes. I rolled my blue eyes. I threw the two police officers. I threw them forward. I looked farther. I saw the two police officers. I saw them flying. I saw them flying backwards. I saw them smashing. I saw them smashed on a wall. I saw them smashed on a heavenly wall. I saw them dropping. I saw them dropped on the ground. I saw them lying on the ground. I saw them bleeding. I saw their blood on the ground. I saw them breathless. I saw them not breathing. I saw them dying. I saw them lifeless. I saw them motionless. I saw them not shaking. I saw them not moving. I saw them dead. I looked farther. I saw police officers. I saw police men. I saw police women. I saw them holding giant guns. I saw them running. I saw them running forward. I saw them running towards me. I saw them shooting. I saw them shooting me. I saw them running and shooting. I saw them shooting me one time. I saw them shooting me two times. I saw them shooting me three times. I saw them shooting me four times. I saw them shooting me five times. I saw them shooting me six times. I saw them shooting me seven times. I saw them shooting me eight times. I saw them shooting me multiple times. I saw nothing. I saw nothing happening. I saw nothing. I saw nothing happening to me. Nothing happened. Nothing happened to me. I grabbed my machine gun. I pointed it at the police officers. I walked. I walked forward. I walked towards the police officers. I shot the police officers. I was walking and shooting. I shot the police officers. I shot all the police men. I shot all the police women. I shot them one time. I shot them two times. I shot them three times. I shot them four times. I shot them five times. I shot them six times. I shot them seven times. I shot them eight times. I shot them multiple times. I shot all the police officers. I assassinated all the police officers. I saw all the police officers. I saw all of them dropping. I saw them dropping. I saw them dropped on the ground. I saw them lying on the ground. I saw them bleeding. I saw their blood on the ground. I saw them breathless. I saw them not breathing. I saw them dying. I saw them motionless. I saw them not shaking. I saw them not moving. I saw them dead. I turned around. I walked. I walked farther. I stood in front of the police gate. I looked at the gate. I rolled my eyes. I rolled my blue eyes. I saw something. I saw something happening. I saw something. I saw something strange. I saw something. I saw something strange happening. I saw the police gate. I saw it opening. I saw it opened. I walked forward. I walked outside the police station. I walked. I walked forward. I walked towards my police motorbike. I stood in front of my motorbike. I jumped on my motorbike. I sat on my motorbike. I placed my machine gun. I placed it inside my pocket. I pushed my hands forward. I grabbed my motorbike. I pushed my feet downwards. I sparked my motorbike. I sparked it one time. I sparked it two times. I sparked it three times. I sparked it multiple times. I saw something. I saw something happening. I saw my motorbike. I saw it running. I saw it running forward. I rode on my motorbike. I rode past the police station. I rode past Florida police station. I rode faster. I rode past car drivers. I rode faster. I rode past motorbike riders. I rode faster. I rode past men driving in cars. I rode faster. I rode past men riding on motorbikes. I rode faster. I rode past women driving in cars. I rode faster. I rode past women riding on motorbikes. I rode faster. I turned around. I saw police cars. I saw police cars chasing me. I placed my hand inside my pocket. I pulled out my machine gun. I grabbed my machine gun. I pointed it at the police cars. I shot the police cars. I shot the police cars one time. I shot the police cars two times. I shot the police cars three times. I shot the police cars four times. I shot the police cars five times. I shot the police cars six times. I shot the police cars seven times. I shot the police cars eight times. I shot the police cars multiple times. I saw the police cars. I saw them blasting. I saw them blasted. I saw the police cars. I saw them busting. I saw them busted. I saw the police cars. I saw them bombing. I saw them bombed. I saw the police cars. I saw them flying. I saw them flying farther. I saw the police cars. I saw them smashing. I saw them smashed on the road. I saw the police cars. I saw them on fire. I saw them burning. I saw them burned. I saw police officers. I saw them riding on motorbikes. I saw the police motorbike riders. I saw Florida police officers. I saw them riding on motorbikes. I saw them chasing me. I saw them pointing their machine guns. I saw them pointing their machine guns at me. I saw them shooting. I saw them shooting me. I saw them shooting me one time. I saw them shooting me two times. I saw them shooting me three times. I saw them shooting me four times. I saw them shooting me five times. I saw them shooting me six times. I saw them shooting me seven times. I saw them shooting me eight times. I saw them shooting me multiple times. I saw nothing. I saw nothing happening. I saw nothing. I saw nothing happening to me. Nothing happened. Nothing happened to me. I looked at the police officers. I looked at the police motorbike riders. I pointed my machine gun. I pointed my giant gun. I pointed it at the police motorbike riders. I shot the police officers. I shot the Florida police officers. I shot them on their motorbikes. I shot them one time. I shot them two times. I shot them three times. I shot them four times. I shot them five times. I shot them six times. I shot them seven times. I shot them eight times. I shot them ten times. I shot them multiple times. I saw the Florida police officers. I saw them flying. I saw them flying farther. I saw them smashing. I saw them smashed on the road. I saw them dropping. I saw them dropped on the road. I saw Florida police officers. I saw them blasted. I saw them bombed. I saw them busted. I saw them lying on the road. I saw them bleeding. I saw them breathless. I saw them not breathing. I saw them motionless. I saw them not shaking. I saw them not moving. I saw them lifeless. I saw them dying. I saw them dead. I looked farther. I saw their police motorbikes. I saw them on fire. I saw them burning. I saw them turning black. I saw them burned. I turned around. I placed my machine gun. I placed my giant gun. I placed it inside my pocket. I pushed my hands forward. I grabbed my motorbike. I pushed my feet downwards. I pushed harder. I rode on my motorbike. I rode faster. I rode past Florida police officers. I rode faster. I rode past dead police officers. I rode faster. I rode past burning police cars. I rode faster. I rode past burned police cars. I rode faster. I rode past burning police motorbikes. I rode faster. I rode past burned police motorbikes. I rode farther. I came across a prison. I came across Florida prison. I parked my motorbike. I parked it in front of the prison. I placed my hand inside my pocket. I pulled out my machine gun. I pulled out my giant gun. I jumped off my motorbike. I walked. I walked forward. I walked towards the prison. I stood in front of the prison gate. I saw the prison gate. I saw it locked. I rolled my eyes. I rolled my blue eyes. I saw something. I saw something happening. I saw something. I saw something strange happening. I saw the prison gate. I saw it opening. I saw it opening faster. I saw it opened. I walked. I walked inside the prison. I saw something. I saw something happening. I saw something. I saw something strange. I saw something. I saw something strange happening. I saw the prison gate. I saw it closing. I saw it closing faster. I walked. I walked farther. I saw a prison officer. I saw him in front of me. I pushed my hand forward. I grabbed him. I grabbed his neck. I grabbed him with one hand. I grabbed his neck with one hand. I raised him. I raised him with one hand. I raised him upwards. I raised him above the sky. I was holding the prison officer. I was holding him with one hand. I looked at him. I smiled. I smiled at the prison officer. I smiled at him. I rolled my eyes. I rolled my blue eyes. I threw him. I threw him farther. I saw the prison officer. I saw him smashing. I saw him smashed on a wall. I saw him smashed on a heavenly wall. I saw him smashed on a prison wall. I saw him dropping. I saw him dropped on the ground. I saw him dropped on a prison ground. I saw him lying on the ground. I saw him dying. I saw him lifeless. I saw him dead. I walked farther. I turned around. I saw a black door. I walked. I walked forward. I walked towards the door. I stood in front of the door. I saw something. I saw the door. I saw it locked. I rolled my eyes. I rolled my blue eyes. I saw something. I saw something happening. I saw something. I saw something strange. I saw something. I saw something strange happening. I saw the door. I saw the black door. I saw it opening. I saw it opening faster. I saw it opened. I walked inside the door. I saw a white man. I saw a prison officer. I saw him sitting on a chair. I saw him wearing a white shirt. I saw him drinking. I saw him drinking vodka. I looked at the prison officer. I pulled out my machine gun. I pointed it at the prison officer. I shot the prison officer. I shot him one time. I shot him two times. I shot him three times. I shot him multiple times. I saw the prison officer. I saw him bleeding. I saw blood on his chest. I saw blood running from his chest. I saw the prison officer. I saw him dying. I saw him breathless. I saw him not breathing. I saw him motionless. I saw him not shaking. I saw him not moving. I saw him dying. I saw him dead. I looked inside his room. I looked on the top of his table. I saw giant keys. I saw the cells keys. I grabbed the giant keys. I grabbed the cells keys. I walked outside his room. I stood in front of his door. I saw his door. I saw it closing. I saw his door closed. I walked farther. I saw the prison officers. I saw them walking. I saw them walking towards me. I saw them shooting. I saw them shooting me. I saw them shooting me one time. I saw them shooting me two times. I saw them shooting me three times. I saw them shooting me multiple times. I saw nothing. I saw nothing happening. I saw nothing happening to me. Nothing happened. Nothing happened to me. I pulled out my machine gun. I shot all the prison officers. I shot them one time. I shot them two times. I shot them three times. I shot them four times. I shot them five times. I shot them six times. I shot them seven times. I shot them eight times. I shot them nine times. I shot them ten times. I shot them multiple times. I shot all the Florida prison officers. I shot all the prison officers. I saw them dropping. I saw them dropping on the ground. I saw them dropped on the ground. I saw them dropped on a prison ground. I saw them breathless. I saw them not breathing. I saw them weakened. I saw them in weakness. I saw them bleeding. I saw their blood on the ground. I saw their blood on a prison ground. I saw them suffering. I saw them in heavy pain. I saw them dying. I saw them motionless. I saw them not shaking. I saw them not moving. I saw them lifeless. I saw them dead. I walked farther. I walked towards a prison cell. I pulled out the cells' keys. I grabbed one cell key. I opened the prison cell. I freed three prisoners. I gave them freedom. I spoke to the three prisoners. I told them to wait outside the prison. I told them to wait for me. I unlocked all the prison gates. I unlocked all the prison cells. I opened all the prisons. I freed all the prisoners. I gave them freedom. I spoke to all the prisoners. I told them to wait outside the prison. I told them to wait for me. I saw all the freed prisoners. I saw them running. I saw them running farther. I saw all the Florida prisoners. I saw them outside the prison. I saw them waiting for me. I walked. I walked farther. I walked outside the prison. I stood in front of the prisoners. I looked farther. I rolled my eyes. I rolled my blue eyes. I saw something. I saw something strange. I saw something. I saw something strange happening. I saw the appearance of motorbikes. I saw hundreds of motorbikes. I saw police motorbikes. I saw them appearing. I saw them in front of the prisoners. I looked at the prisoners. I saw them looking at me. I saw them speaking. I saw them speaking to me. I saw them thanking me. I saw them saluting me. I saw the Florida prisoners. I saw them looking at me. I saw them saying something. I saw them saying something to me. I saw them saying goodbye. I saw them saying goodbye to me. I saw them walking. I saw them walking forward. I saw them walking towards the police motorbikes. I saw them in front of the motorbikes. I saw them jumping on the motorbikes. I saw them sitting on the motorbikes. I saw them pushing their hands forward. I saw them grabbing their motorbikes. I saw them pushing their feet downwards. I saw them pushing harder. I saw them sparking. I saw them sparking their motorbikes. I saw them sparking it the first time. I saw them sparking it the second time. I saw them sparking it the third time. I saw them sparking it multiple times. I saw the Florida prisoners. I saw them riding. I saw them riding on their motorbikes. I saw them riding faster. I saw them riding past the prison. I saw them riding faster. I saw them riding past me. I saw the Florida prisoners. I saw them riding farther. I saw them riding back home. I walked. I walked forward. I walked towards my police motorbike. I stood in front of my police motorbike. I jumped on my police motorbike. I sat on my motorbike. I placed my machine gun. I placed my giant gun. I placed it inside my pocket. I pushed my hands forward. I grabbed my motorbike. I pushed my feet downwards. I pushed harder. I sparked my motorbike. I sparked it the first time. I sparked it the second time. I sparked it the third time. I sparked it multiple times. I rode on my motorbike. I rode faster. I rode past Florida prison. I rode faster. I rode past police cars. I rode faster. I rode past police motorbikes. I rode farther. I came across somewhere. I came across another state. I came across another East coast state.

4

THE ASSASSINATION MAN's JOURNEY

FROM

FLORIDA SOUTH CAROLINA

I rode on my police motorbike. I rode it in South Carolina. I rode faster. I rode past men riding on motorbikes. I rode faster. I rode past women riding on motorbikes. I rode faster. I rode past men driving in cars. I rode faster. I rode past women driving in cars. I rode faster. I rode past police men riding on motorbikes. I rode faster. I rode past police men driving in cars. I rode faster. I rode past police women riding on motorbikes. I rode faster. I rode past police women driving in cars. I rode faster. I rode past police men riding on police motorbikes. I rode faster. I rode past police men driving in police cars. I rode faster. I rode past police women riding on police motorbikes. I rode faster. I rode past police women driving in police cars. I rode faster. I rode past South Carolina train stations. I rode farther. I came across a police station. I came across South Carolina police station. I parked my police motorbike. I parked it in front of South Carolina police station. I pushed my hand downwards. I pushed my hand inside my pocket. I pulled out my machine gun. I grabbed my giant gun. I jumped off my police motorbike. I walked. I walked forward. I walked towards the police station. I stood in front of the police station. I stood in front of South Carolina police station. I stood in front of a giant gate. I looked at the giant gate. I rolled my eyes. I rolled my blue eyes. I saw something. I saw something strange. I saw something. I saw something happening. I saw something. I saw something strange happening. I saw the giant gate. I saw it opening. I saw it opening faster. I saw it opened. I walked inside the giant gate. I saw the giant gate. I saw it closing. I saw it closing faster. I saw it closed. I walked inside the police station. I walked farther. I saw a police man. I saw one police officer. I saw him walking. I saw him walking towards me. I walked. I walked forward. I walked towards the police man. I stood in front of the police officer. I pushed my hand forward. I pushed harder. I grabbed the police man. I grabbed him with one hand. I grabbed him on his neck. I raised the police officer. I raised him with one hand. I raised him upwards. I raised him above the sky. I looked at the police man. I rolled my eyes. I rolled my blue eyes. I smiled. I smiled at the police man. I smiled at the police officer. I threw the police man. I threw the police officer. I threw him forward. I saw the police man. I saw the police officer. I saw him flying. I saw him flying backwards. I saw him smashing. I saw him smashed on a wall. I saw him smashed on a giant wall. I saw him smashed on a heavenly wall. I saw the police man. I saw the police officer. I saw him dropping. I saw him dropped on the ground. I saw him dropped on a police ground. I saw him bleeding. I saw his blood on the ground. I saw his blood on a police ground. I saw him weakened. I saw him in weakness. I saw him suffering. I saw him in heavy pain. I looked farther. I saw the police man. I saw a painful police man. I saw him rising. I saw him rising on the ground. I saw him rising upwards. I saw him upwards. I saw him standing. I saw him standing upwards. I saw him pushing his hand. I saw him pushing his hand inside his pocket. I saw him pulling out his gun. I saw him pulling out a giant gun. I saw him grabbing his machine gun. I saw him grabbing his giant gun. I saw him walking. I saw him walking towards me. I saw him walking forward. I saw him shooting. I saw him walking and shooting. I saw him shooting me. I saw him shooting me one time. I saw him shooting me two times. I saw him shooting me three times. I saw him shooting me four times. I saw him shooting me five times. I saw him shooting me six times. I saw him shooting me seven times. I saw him shooting me eight times. I saw him shooting me nine times. I saw him shooting me ten times. I saw him shooting me multiple times. I saw nothing. I saw nothing happening. I saw nothing. I saw nothing happening to me. Nothing happened to me. I saw the police man. I saw him in front of me. I grabbed him. I grabbed him with one hand. I grabbed his neck. I raised the police officer. I raised him with one hand. I raised him upwards. I raised him above the sky. I looked at the police man. I looked at the police officer. I smiled. I smiled at the police man. I smiled at the police officer. I rolled my eyes. I rolled my blue eyes. I threw the police man. I threw the police officer. I threw him forward. I looked farther. I saw the police man. I saw the police officer. I saw him flying. I saw him flying backwards. I saw him smashing. I saw him smashed on a wall. I saw him smashed on a heavenly wall. I saw him smashed on a police wall. I saw him dropping. I saw him dropped on the ground. I saw him lying on the ground. I saw him bleeding. I saw his blood on the ground. I saw his blood on a police ground. I saw him breathless. I saw him weakened. I saw him in weakness. I saw him suffering. I saw him in heavy pain. I saw him dying. I saw him motionless. I saw him not shaking. I saw him not moving. I saw him lifeless. I saw him dead. I walked. I walked inside the police station. I walked farther. I turned around. I saw a lot of police men. I saw them walking. I saw them walking towards me. I saw a lot of police officers. I saw them holding machine guns. I saw them holding giant guns. I saw them shooting. I saw them shooting me. I saw them shooting me one time. I saw them shooting me two times. I saw them shooting me three times. I saw them shooting me four times. I saw them shooting me five times. I saw them shooting me six times. I saw them shooting me seven times. I saw them shooting me eight times. I saw them shooting me nine times. I saw them shooting me ten times. I saw them shooting me multiple times. I saw nothing. I saw nothing happening. I saw nothing. I saw nothing happening to me. Nothing happened. Nothing happened to me. I pulled out my machine gun. I grabbed my giant gun. I pointed it forward. I pointed it at the police men. I shot the police men. I shot all the police men. I shot them one time. I shot them two times. I shot them three times. I shot them four times. I shot them five times. I shot them six times. I shot them seven times. I shot them eight times. I shot them nine times. I shot them ten times. I shot them multiple times. I saw the police men. I saw the police officers. I saw South Carolina police men. I saw South Carolina police officers. I saw them dropping. I saw them dropped on the ground. I saw them dropped on a police ground. I saw them lying on the ground. I saw them lying on a police ground. I saw them bleeding. I saw their blood. I saw their blood on the ground. I saw their blood on a police ground. I saw them dying. I saw them dying on the ground. I saw them dying on a police ground. I saw them dead. I saw them dead on the ground. I saw them dead on a police ground. I walked. I walked inside the police station. I walked farther. I saw a lot of police women. I saw a lot of South Carolina police women. I saw them walking. I saw them walking forward. I saw them walking towards me. I saw them holding giant guns. I saw them shooting. I saw them walking and shooting. I saw them shooting me. I saw them shooting me one time. I saw them shooting me two times. I saw them shooting me three times. I saw them shooting me four times. I saw them shooting me five times. I saw them shooting me six times. I saw them shooting me seven times. I saw them shooting me eight times. I saw them shooting me nine times. I saw them shooting me ten times. I saw them shooting me multiple times. I saw nothing. I saw nothing happening. I saw nothing. I saw nothing happening to me. Nothing happened. Nothing happened to me. I grabbed my machine gun. I grabbed my giant gun. I pointed it at the police women. I pointed it at South Carolina police women. I shot the police women. I shot the police officers. I shot them one time. I shot them two times. I shot them three times. I shot them four times. I shot them five times. I shot them six times. I shot them seven times. I shot them eight times. I shot them nine times. I shot them ten times. I shot them multiple times. I saw the police women. I saw the South Carolina police women. I saw all the police women. I saw all the South Carolina police officers. I saw all of them dropping. I saw them dropping. I saw them dropped. I saw them dropped on the ground. I saw them dropped on a police ground. I saw them lying on the ground. I saw them lying on a police ground. I saw them bleeding. I saw their blood on the ground. I saw their blood on a police ground. I saw them breathless. I saw them not breathing. I saw them weakened. I saw them in weakness. I saw them suffering. I saw them in heavy pain. I saw them dying. I saw them motionless. I saw them not shaking. I saw them not moving. I saw them lifeless. I saw them dead. I saw them dead on the ground. I saw them dead on a police ground. I walked farther. I stood in front of all the police gates. I rolled my eyes. I rolled my blue eyes. I opened all the police gates. I walked. I walked outside the police station. I walked forward. I walked towards my police motorbike. I stood in front of my police motorbike. I jumped on my motorbike. I sat on my motorbike. I pushed my hand downwards. I placed my machine gun. I placed it inside my pocket. I pushed my hand forward. I grabbed my motorbike. I pushed my feet downwards. I pushed it harder. I pushed it one time. I pushed it two times. I pushed it three times. I pushed it multiple times. I saw my motorbike. I saw it sparking. I saw it sparking the first time. I saw it sparking the second time. I saw it sparking the third time. I saw it sparking multiple times. I saw my motorbike. I saw it sparked. I rode on my motorbike. I rode with my head downwards. I rode faster. I rode past South Carolina police station. I rode farther. I turned around. I saw police cars. I saw South Carolina police cars. I saw them chasing me. I saw South Carolina police officers. I saw them driving police cars. I saw them chasing me. I saw them looking outside their car windows. I saw them pulling out their guns. I saw them pointing out their giant guns. I saw them shooting. I saw them shooting me. I saw them shooting me one time. I saw them shooting me two times. I saw them shooting me three times. I saw them shooting me four times. I saw them shooting me five times. I saw them shooting me six times. I saw them shooting me seven times. I saw them shooting me eight times. I saw them shooting me nine times. I saw them shooting me ten times. I saw them shooting me multiple times. I saw nothing. I saw nothing happening. I saw nothing. I saw nothing happening to me. Nothing happened. Nothing happened to me. I pushed my hand inside my pocket. I pulled out my machine gun. I grabbed my giant gun. I pointed it at the police officers. I pointed it at the police cars. I shot the police officers. I shot the police men. I shot the police women. I shot the police officers one time. I shot the police officers two times. I shot the police officers three times. I shot the police officers multiple times. I shot the police cars. I shot the police cars one time. I shot the police cars two times. I shot the police cars three times. I shot the police cars multiple times. I saw the police cars. I saw it flying. I saw it flying backwards. I saw the police cars. I saw it rolling. I saw it rolling like a rollercoaster. I saw it smashing. I saw it smashed on the road. I saw it dropping. I saw it dropped on a road. I saw the police cars. I saw it blasting. I saw busting. I saw it bombing. I saw it bombed. I saw it bombed on a road. I saw it on fire. I saw it burning. I saw it burned. I saw South Carolina police men. I saw South Carolina police women. I saw them riding. I saw them riding on motorbikes. I saw them chasing me. I saw them pulling out their giant guns. I saw them pointing their guns. I saw them pointing their giant guns. I saw them pointing their guns at me. I saw them shooting. I saw them shooting me. I saw them shooting me one time. I saw them shooting me two times. I saw them shooting me three times. I saw them shooting me multiple times. I saw nothing. I saw nothing happening. I saw nothing. I saw nothing happening to me. Nothing happened. Nothing happened to me. I grabbed my machine gun. I pointed it at the police men. I pointed it at the police women. I pointed it at South Carolina police men. I pointed it at South Carolina police women. I shot the police men. I shot the police women. I shot the South Carolina police officers. I shot them on their motorbikes. I shot them one time. I shot them two times. I shot them three times. I shot them multiple times. I saw the police men. I saw the police women. I saw the South Carolina police officers. I saw them flying. I saw them flying from their motorbikes. I saw them flying backwards. I saw them dropping. I saw them dropped on the ground. I saw them dropped on a road. I saw their motorbikes. I saw their motorbikes flying. I saw their motorbike smashing on the ground. I saw their motorbikes smashing on a road. I saw their motorbikes. I saw their motorbikes dropping. I saw their motorbikes dropping on a road. I saw their motorbikes rolling. I saw their motorbikes blasting. I saw their motorbikes busting. I saw their motorbikes bombing. I saw their motorbikes on fire. I saw their motorbikes burning. I saw their motorbikes. I saw them bombing. I saw them burning. I saw them burned. I looked farther. I saw the South Carolina police men. I saw the South Carolina police women. I saw the South Carolina police officers. I saw them lying on the ground. I saw them lying on a road. I saw them bleeding. I saw their blood on the ground. I saw their blood on the road. I saw them breathless. I saw them not breathing. I saw them motionless. I saw them not shaking. I saw them not moving. I saw them dying. I saw them lifeless. I saw them dead. I saw them dead on the ground. I saw them dead on the road. I turned around. I grabbed my motorbike. I rode faster. I rode past the South Carolina police officers. I rode past the dead police officers. I rode past the dead police men. I rode past the dead police women. I rode faster. I rode past the burning police motorbikes. I rode past the burned police motorbikes. I rode faster. I rode past the burning police cars. I rode past the burned police cars. I rode farther. I came across a prison. I came across a prison in South Carolina. I parked my police motorbike. I parked it in front of the prison. I pushed my hand downwards. I pushed my hand inside my pocket. I pulled out my machine gun. I grabbed my giant gun. I jumped off my motorbike. I walked. I walked forward. I walked towards the prison. I stood in front of the prison. I stood in front of the prison gate. I saw the prison gate. I saw it closed. I looked at the prison gate. I rolled my eyes. I rolled my blue eyes. I saw something. I saw something strange. I saw something. I saw something strange happening. I saw the prison gate. I saw it opening. I saw it opening faster. I saw it opened. I walked. I walked inside the prison. I walked forward. I walked farther. I saw a prison man. I saw a prison officer. I saw him walking. I saw him walking towards me. I saw him walking forward. I saw him in front of me. I pushed my hand forward. I grabbed the prison man. I grabbed his neck. I grabbed him with one hand. I raised him upwards. I raised him above the sky. I looked at the prison officer. I rolled my eyes. I rolled my blue eyes. I smiled. I smiled at him. I threw him. I threw him forward. I saw the prison man. I saw the prison officer. I saw him flying. I saw him flying backwards. I saw him smashing. I saw him smashed on a wall. I saw him smashed on a heavenly wall. I saw him smashed on a prison wall. I saw him dropping. I saw him dropped on a prison wall. I saw him lying on the ground. I saw him lying on a prison ground. I saw him bleeding. I saw his blood. I saw his blood on the ground. I saw his blood on a prison ground. I saw him dying. I saw him breathless. I saw him not breathing. I saw him motionless. I saw him not shaking. I saw him not moving. I saw him lifeless. I saw him dead. I saw him dead on the ground. I saw him dead on a prison ground. I walked forward. I walked farther. I walked towards the dead man. I walked towards the dead prison officer. I stood in front of the dead man. I stood in front of the dead prison officer. I pushed my hand downwards. I searched the prison officer. I placed my hand inside his pocket. I pulled out something. I pulled out the prison keys. I pulled out the cells' keys. I grabbed the prison keys. I grabbed the cells' keys. I turned around. I walked forward. I walked farther. I opened all the prison gates. I walked. I walked forward. I walked farther. I walked towards the prison cells. I placed the keys inside all the prison cells. I opened all the prison cells. I freed all the prisoners. I freed all the South Carolina prisoners. I gave freedom to all the prisoners. I gave all the prisoners freedom. I spoke to all the prisoners. I told all the prisoners to walk outside the prison. I told them to wait outside the prison. I told all of them to wait for me. I told all of them to wait for me outside the prison. I saw all the prisoners. I saw all of them walking. I saw them walking outside. I saw them outside the South Carolina prison. I saw them waiting. I saw them waiting for me. I walked forward. I walked farther. I walked outside the prison. I walked outside the South Carolina prison. I walked forward. I stood in front of the prisoners. I looked forward. I rolled my eyes. I rolled my blue eyes. I saw something. I saw something strange. I saw something. I saw something strange happening. I saw the appearance of motorbikes. I saw hundreds of motorbikes. I saw it appearing. I saw it appeared in front of me. I turned around. I looked at the prisoners. I spoke to the prisoners. I told them to ride on the motorbikes. I told them to ride back home. I saw the prisoners. I saw them looking at me. I saw them speaking. I saw them speaking to me. I saw them thanking me. I saw them giving me thanksgiving. I saw them saying goodbye. I saw them saying goodbye to Peter Erickson. I saw them saying goodbye to me. I saw the South Carolina prisoners. I saw them walking. I saw them walking forward. I saw them walking towards the motorbikes. I saw them in front of the motorbikes. I saw them grabbing the motorbikes. I saw them jumping on the motorbikes. I saw them sitting on the motorbikes. I saw them pushing their hands forward. I saw them grabbing their motorbikes. I saw them pushing their feet downwards. I saw them pushing harder. I saw them sparking. I saw them sparking their motorbikes. I saw them sparking one time. I saw them sparking two times. I saw them sparking three times. I saw them sparking multiple times. I saw them riding. I saw them riding on their motorbikes. I saw them riding faster. I saw them riding past me. I saw them riding past the South Carolina prison. I saw them riding farther. I saw them riding back home. I walked forward. I walked towards my police motorbike. I stood in front of my police motorbike. I jumped on my motorbike. I sat on my motorbike. I grabbed my machine gun. I was holding my machine gun. I pushed my hand downwards. I placed my machine gun. I placed my giant gun. I placed it inside my pocket. I pushed my hands forward. I pushed my feet downwards. I pushed harder. I sparked my motorbike. I sparked it one time. I sparked it two times. I sparked it three times. I sparked it multiple times. I rode on my motorbike. I rode faster. I rode past the South Carolina prison. I rode faster. I rode past South Carolina police cars. I rode faster. I rode past South Carolina police motorbikes. I rode farther. I came across somewhere. I came across another state. I came across another East coast state.

5

THE ASSASSINATION MAN's JOURNEY

FROM SOUTH CAROLINA TO NORTH CAROLINA I rode on my motorbike. I rode in North Carolina. I rode faster. I rode past police cars. I rode faster. I rode past police motorbikes. I rode faster. I rode past men riding on motorbikes. I rode faster. I rode past men driving in cars. I rode faster. I rode past women riding on motorbikes. I rode faster. I rode past women driving in cars. I rode faster. I rode past train stations. I rode farther. I came across somewhere. I came across a police station. I came across North Carolina police station. I parked my police motorbike. I parked it in front of the police station. I pushed my hand inside my pocket. I pulled out my machine gun. I grabbed my giant gun. I jumped off my motorbike. I walked forward. I walked towards the police station. I stood in front of the police station. I stood in front of a gate. I stood in front of a giant gate. I looked at the giant gate. I saw the giant gate. I saw it locked. I looked at it. I rolled my eyes. I rolled my blue eyes. I saw something. I saw something happening. I saw something. I saw something strange. I saw something. I saw something strange happening. I saw the giant gate. I saw it opening. I saw it opening faster. I saw it opening faster like a warrior. I saw it opened. I walked inside the police station. I walked forward. I walked farther. I saw one police man. I saw a police man. I saw him walking. I saw him walking forward. I saw him walking towards me. I grabbed my machine gun. I pointed it at the police man. I pointed it at the police officer. I shot the police man. I shot the police officer. I shot him one time. I shot him two times. I shot him three times. I shot him multiple times. I saw the police man. I saw the police officer. I saw the North Carolina police man. I saw nothing. I saw nothing happening. I saw nothing. I saw nothing happening to him. I saw the North Carolina police officer. I saw nothing. I saw nothing happening. I saw nothing. I saw nothing happening to him. I saw the police man. I saw the police officer. I saw him pulling out his gun. I saw him pulling out a giant gun. I saw him walking. I saw him walking forward. I saw him walking towards me. I saw him shooting. I saw him walking and shooting. I saw him shooting me. I saw him shooting me one time. I saw him shooting me two times. I saw him shooting me three times. I saw him shooting me multiple times. I saw nothing. I saw nothing happening. I saw nothing. I saw nothing happening to me. I saw the police man. I saw the police officer. I saw him in front of me. I looked at him. I pushed my hand forward. I grabbed him. I grabbed him with one hand. I grabbed his neck. I grabbed his neck with one hand. I raised him. I raised him with one hand. I raised him upwards. I raised him above the sky. I was holding him. I was holding him with one hand. I looked at him. I smiled. I smiled and I smiled again. I smiled at the police man. I smiled at the police officer. I smiled at the North Carolina police man. I smiled at the North Carolina police officer. I looked at the police man. I looked at the police officer. I rolled my eyes. I rolled my blue eyes. I threw the police man. I threw him forward. I saw the police man. I saw him flying. I saw him flying backwards. I saw him smashing. I saw him smashed on a wall. I saw him smashed on a heavenly wall. I saw him smashed on a police wall. I saw him dropping. I saw him dropped on the ground. I saw him dropped on a police ground. I looked farther. I saw the police man. I saw the police officer. I saw him lying on the ground. I saw him lying on a police ground. I saw him bleeding. I saw his blood on the ground. I saw his blood on a police ground. I saw him dying. I saw him breathless. I saw him not breathing. I saw him weakened. I saw him in weakness. I saw him suffering. I saw him in heavy pain. I saw him motionless. I saw him not shaking. I saw him not moving. I saw him dead. I walked forward. I walked past the police man. I walked past the dead police man. I walked past the police officer. I walked past the dead police officer. I walked farther. I saw a lot of police officers. I saw a lot of police men. I saw them walking. I saw them walking forward. I saw them walking towards me. I saw them pulling out their giant guns. I saw them pointing their guns. I saw them pointing their guns at me. I saw them shooting. I saw them shooting me. I saw them shooting me one time. I saw them shooting me two times. I saw them shooting me three times. I saw them shooting me four times. I saw them shooting me five times. I saw them shooting me six times. I saw them shooting me seven times. I saw them shooting me eight times. I saw them shooting me nine times. I saw them shooting me ten times. I saw them shooting me multiple times. I saw nothing. I saw nothing happening. I saw nothing. I saw nothing happening to me. I pulled out my machine gun. I grabbed my giant gun. I pointed it at the police men. I shot the police men. I shot the North Carolina police men. I shot the police officers. I shot the North Carolina police officers. I shot them one time. I shot them two times. I shot them three times. I shot them four times. I shot them five times. I shot them six times. I shot them seven times. I shot them eight times. I shot them nine times. I shot them ten times. I shot them multiple times. I saw all the police men. I saw them dropping. I saw them dropped on the ground. I saw them dropped on a police ground. I saw them bleeding. I saw their blood. I saw their blood on the ground. I saw their blood on a police ground. I saw them dying. I saw them weakened. I saw them in weakness. I saw them breathless. I saw them not breathing. I saw them suffering. I saw them in heavy pain. I saw them motionless. I saw them not shaking. I saw them not moving. I saw dying police officers. I saw dying police men. I saw them dead. I saw them dead on the ground. I saw them dead on a blood-filled ground. I saw them dead on a police ground. I walked forward. I walked past the dead police men. I walked farther. I saw a lot of police women. I saw them walking. I saw them walking forward. I saw them walking towards me. I saw them pulling out their giant guns. I saw them holding their giant guns. I saw them pointing their giant guns. I saw them pointing their guns forward. I saw them pointing their guns at me. I saw them shooting. I saw them walking and shooting. I saw them shooting me. I saw them shooting me one time. I saw them shooting me two times. I saw them shooting me three times. I saw them shooting me four times. I saw them shooting me five times. I saw them shooting me six times. I saw them shooting me seven times. I saw them shooting me eight times. I saw them shooting me nine times. I saw them shooting me ten times. I saw them shooting me multiple times. I saw nothing. I saw nothing happening. I saw nothing. I saw nothing happening to me. I grabbed my machine gun. I pointed it at the police women. I shot the police women. I shot them one time. I shot them two times. I shot them three times. I shot them four times. I shot them five times. I shot them six times. I shot them seven times. I shot them eight times. I shot them nine times. I shot them ten times. I shot them multiple times. I saw all the police women. I saw them dropping. I saw them dropped. I saw them dropped on the ground. I saw them dropped on a police ground. I saw them bleeding. I saw their blood. I saw their blood on the ground. I saw their blood on a blood-filled ground. I saw their blood on a police ground. I looked forward. I looked on the ground. I looked on a police ground. I saw dying police women. I saw them weakened. I saw them in weakness. I saw them suffering. I saw them in heavy pain. I saw them breathless. I saw them not breathing. I saw them motionless. I saw them not shaking. I saw them not moving. I saw the North Carolina police women. I saw them dead. I saw them dead on the ground. I saw them dead on a police ground. I walked forward. I walked past the police women. I walked past the dead police women. I walked farther. I walked outside the police station. I walked outside the North Carolina police station. I walked forward. I walked towards my motorbike. I stood in front of my police motorbike. I jumped on my motorbike. I sat on my police motorbike. I grabbed my machine gun. I pushed it inside my pocket. I pushed my hands forward. I grabbed my motorbike. I pushed my feet downwards. I pushed harder. I sparked my motorbike. I sparked it one time. I sparked it two times. I sparked it three times. I sparked it multiple times. I rode on my motorbike. I rode faster. I rode past the police station. I rode past North Carolina police station. I rode faster. I turned around. I looked backwards. I saw a lot of police cars. I saw a lot of police cars chasing me. I saw police men. I saw North Carolina police men. I saw North Carolina police women. I saw them driving police cars. I saw them driving in police cars. I saw them chasing me. I saw them pulling out their giant guns. I saw them pointing their giant guns outside their car windows. I saw them pointing their giant guns at me. I saw them shooting. I saw them shooting me. I saw them shooting me one time. I saw them shooting me two times. I saw them shooting me three times. I saw them shooting me four times. I saw them shooting me five times. I saw them shooting me six times. I saw them shooting me seven times. I saw them shooting me eight times. I saw them shooting me nine times. I saw them shooting me ten times. I saw them shooting me multiple times. I saw nothing. I saw nothing happening. I saw nothing. I saw nothing happening to me. I grabbed my giant gun. I pointed it at the police cars. I shot the police cars. I shot the police cars one time. I shot the police cars two times. I shot the police cars three times. I shot the police cars four times. I shot the police cars five times. I shot the police cars six times. I shot the police cars seven times. I shot the police cars eight times. I shot the police cars nine times. I shot the police cars ten times. I shot the police cars multiple times. I saw something. I saw something happening. I saw something. I saw something strange. I saw something. I saw something strange happening. I saw the police cars. I saw them rolling. I saw them rolling backwards. I saw them smashing. I saw them smashed on the ground. I saw them smashed on a road. I saw them dropping. I saw them dropped on a road. I saw them blasting. I saw them blasted. I saw them busting. I saw them busted. I saw them bombing. I saw them bombed. I saw them on fire. I saw them burning. I saw them burned. I turned around. I rode on my motorbike. I rode faster. I rode past burning police cars. I rode past burned police cars. I rode faster. I turned around. I looked backwards. I saw North Carolina police men. I saw North Carolina police women. I saw them riding on police motorbikes. I saw them riding faster. I saw them chasing me. I saw them pulling out their giant guns. I saw them grabbing their giant guns. I saw them pointing their giant guns. I saw them pointing their guns forward. I saw them pointing their guns at me. I saw them shooting. I saw them shooting me. I saw them shooting me one time. I saw them shooting me two times. I saw them shooting me three times. I saw them shooting me four times. I saw them shooting me five times. I saw them shooting me six times. I saw them shooting me seven times. I saw them shooting me eight times. I saw them shooting me nine times. I saw them shooting me ten times. I saw them shooting me multiple times. I saw nothing. I saw nothing happening. I saw nothing. I saw nothing happening to me. I grabbed my machine gun. I pointed it at the police men. I pointed it at the North Carolina police men. I pointed it at the police women. I pointed it at the North Carolina police women. I pointed it at the North Carolina police officers. I shot the police men. I shot the police women. I shot the North Carolina police officers. I shot them on their motorbikes. I shot them one time. I shot them two times. I shot them three times. I shot them four times. I shot them five times. I shot them six times. I shot them seven times. I shot them eight times. I shot them nine times. I shot them ten times. I shot them multiple times. I saw something. I saw something happening. I saw the police men. I saw the police women. I saw them flying. I saw them flying from their motorbikes. I saw them flying backwards. I saw them smashing. I saw them smashed on the ground. I saw them dropping. I saw them dropped on the ground. I saw them lying on the ground. I saw them lying on a road. I saw them bleeding. I saw their blood on a road. I saw them dying. I saw them breathless. I saw them not breathing. I saw them suffering. I saw them in heavy pain. I looked farther. I saw the police men. I saw the police women. I saw them dead. I saw them dead on the ground. I saw them dead on a road. I turned around. I grabbed my motorbike. I rode faster. I rode past the dead police men. I rode past the dead police women. I rode past dead police officers. I rode past their police motorbikes. I rode past burning motorbikes. I rode past burned motorbikes. I rode farther. I came across somewhere. I came across a prison. I came across a prison in North Carolina. I came across a North Carolina prison. I parked my police motorbike. I parked it in front of the prison. I grabbed my machine gun. I grabbed my giant gun. I jumped off my motorbike. I walked. I walked forward. I walked towards the prison. I stood in front of the prison. I stood in front of a giant gate. I saw the prison gate. I saw a giant gate. I saw it locked. I looked at the giant gate. I looked at it. I rolled my eyes. I rolled my blue eyes. I saw something. I saw something happening. I saw something. I saw something strange. I saw something. I saw something strange happening. I saw the giant gate. I saw it opening. I saw it opened. I walked inside the prison. I walked farther. I saw one prison officer. I saw one prison man. I saw him walking. I saw him walking forward. I saw him walking towards me. I pulled out my giant gun. I grabbed my giant gun. I pointed it at the prison officer. I shot the prison man. I shot the prison officer. I shot him one time. I shot him two times. I shot him three times. I shot him multiple times. I saw him dropping. I saw him dropped on the ground. I saw him dropped on a prison ground. I saw him dying. I saw him bleeding. I saw his blood on the ground. I saw his blood on a blood-filled ground. I saw his blood on a prison ground. I saw him breathless. I saw him not breathing. I saw him motionless. I saw him not shaking. I saw him not moving. I saw him dead. I saw him dead on the ground. I saw him dead on a prison ground. I walked. I walked forward. I walked towards him. I stood in front of him. I looked at him. I pushed my hand downwards. I grabbed him. I rolled him. I rolled him from the left to the right. I searched him. I placed my hand inside his pocket. I pulled out something. I pulled out some keys. I pulled out the prisoners' keys. I pulled out the cells' keys. I grabbed myself upwards. I walked. I walked farther. I saw a lot of male prison officers. I saw them walking. I saw them walking forward. I saw them walking towards me. I saw them pulling out their giant guns. I saw them pointing their guns forward. I saw them pointing their guns at me. I saw them shooting. I saw them walking and shooting. I saw them shooting me. I saw them shooting me one time. I saw them shooting me two times. I saw them shooting me three times. I saw them shooting me four times. I saw them shooting me five times. I saw them shooting me six times. I saw them shooting me seven times. I saw them shooting me eight times. I saw them shooting me nine times. I saw them shooting me ten times. I saw them shooting me multiple times. I saw nothing. I saw nothing happening. I saw nothing. I saw nothing happening to me. I pulled out my giant gun. I grabbed it. I pointed it forward. I pointed it at the male prison officers. I shot the prison male officers. I shot them one time. I shot them two times. I shot them three times. I shot them four times. I shot them five times. I shot them six times. I shot them seven times. I shot them eight times. I shot them nine times. I shot them ten times. I shot them multiple times. I saw all the male prison officers. I saw them dropping. I saw them dropped on the ground. I saw them dropped on a prison ground. I saw them lying on the ground. I saw them lying on a prison ground. I saw them bleeding. I saw their blood on the ground. I saw their blood on a blood-filled ground. I saw their blood on a prison ground. I saw them dying. I saw them breathless. I saw them not breathing. I saw them motionless. I saw them not shaking. I saw them not moving. I saw them dead. I saw them dead on the ground. I saw them dead on a blood-filled ground. I saw them dead on a prison ground. I walked. I walked forward. I walked past dead prison male officers. I walked farther. I saw the female prison officers. I saw them farther. I saw them running. I saw them running forward. I saw them running towards me. I saw them pulling out their giant guns. I saw them pointing their guns. I saw them pointing their giant guns. I saw them pointing their guns at me. I saw them running. I saw them shooting. I saw them running and shooting. I saw them shooting me. I saw them shooting me one time. I saw them shooting me two times. I saw them shooting me three times. I saw them shooting me four times. I saw them shooting me five times. I saw them shooting me six times. I saw them shooting me seven times. I saw them shooting me eight times. I saw them shooting me nine times. I saw them shooting me ten times. I saw them shooting me multiple times. I saw nothing. I saw nothing happening. I saw nothing. I saw nothing happening to me. I pulled out my machine gun. I grabbed my giant gun. I pointed it forward. I pointed it at the prison female officers. I shot the prison female officers. I shot them one time. I shot them two times. I shot them three times. I shot them four times. I shot them five times. I shot them six times. I shot them seven times. I shot them eight times. I shot them nine times. I shot them ten times. I shot them multiple times. I saw all the prison female officers. I saw them dropping. I saw them dropped. I saw them dropped on the ground. I saw them dropped on a prison ground. I saw them lying on the ground. I saw them lying on a prison ground. I saw them bleeding. I saw their blood. I saw their blood on the ground. I saw their blood on a blood-filled ground. I saw their blood on a prison ground. I saw them dying. I saw them weakened. I saw them in weakness. I saw them suffering. I saw them in heavy pain. I saw them breathless. I saw them not breathing. I saw them motionless. I saw them not shaking. I saw them not moving. I saw the prison female officers. I saw them dead. I saw them dead on the ground. I saw them dead on a blood-filled ground. I saw them dead on a prison ground. I walked. I walked forward. I walked past the dead prison officers. I walked farther. I opened all the prison gates. I walked farther. I opened all the cells. I opened all the cell doors. I freed all the prisoners. I freed all the North Carolina prisoners. I gave all the prisoners freedom. I spoke to all the freed prisoners. I told all of them to wait outside. I told all of them to wait outside the prison. I told all of them to wait for me. I told all of them to wait outside the prison for me. I saw all the freed prisoners. I saw all of them running. I saw all of them running outside. I saw all of them outside the prison. I saw all of them waiting outside the prison. I saw all of them waiting for me. I walked. I walked farther. I walked outside North Carolina prison. I walked outside the prison. I walked forward. I stood in front of the freed prisoners. I looked forward. I rolled my eyes. I rolled my blue eyes. I saw something. I saw something happening. I saw something. I saw something strange. I saw something. I saw something strange happening. I saw the appearance of motorbikes. I saw hundreds of police motorbikes. I saw them appearing. I saw them in front of me. I turned around. I faced forward. I looked at the freed prisoners. I spoke to the freed prisoners. I told them to jump on the police motorbikes. I told them to ride back home. I looked at the freed prisoners. I saw them looking at me. I saw them speaking. I saw them speaking to me. I saw them thanking me. I saw them thanking me for giving them freedom. I saw them giving thanksgiving. I saw them thanking me. I saw all the freed prisoners. I saw them saying goodbye. I saw them saying goodbye to Peter Erickson. I saw them saying goodbye to the assassination man. I saw them saying goodbye to me. I saw the freed prisoners. I saw them walking forward. I saw them walking towards the police motorbikes. I saw them in front of hundred motorbikes. I saw them in front of hundred police motorbikes. I saw them jumping on the police motorbikes. I saw them sitting on the motorbikes. I saw them pushing their hands forward. I saw them grabbing the motorbikes. I saw them pushing their feet downwards. I saw them pushing harder. I saw them sparking their motorbikes. I saw them sparking one time. I saw them sparking two times. I saw them sparking three times. I saw them sparking multiple times. I saw them riding. I saw them riding on the police motorbikes. I saw them riding faster. I saw them riding past me. I saw them riding past the North Carolina prison. I saw them riding farther. I saw them riding back home. I walked. I walked forward. I walked towards my police motorbike. I stood in front of my motorbike. I jumped on my motorbike. I sat on my motorbike. I placed my machine gun. I placed it inside my pocket. I pushed my hands forward. I grabbed my motorbike. I pushed my feet downwards. I pushed harder. I sparked my police motorbike. I sparked it one time. I sparked it two times. I sparked it three times. I sparked it multiple times. I rode on my motorbike. I rode faster. I rode past the North Carolina prison. I rode faster. I rode past police cars. I rode faster. I rode past police motorbikes. I rode faster. I rode past train stations. I rode faster. I rode past men riding on motorbikes. I rode faster. I rode past women riding on motorbikes. I rode faster. I rode past men driving in cars. I rode faster. I rode past women driving in cars. I rode farther. I came across another State. I came across another East coast state.

6

THE ASSASSINATION MAN's JOURNEY

FROM NORTH CAROLINA TO GEORGIA

I rode on my police motorbike. I rode faster. I rode inside Georgia. I rode faster. I rode in Georgia. I rode faster. I rode past men driving in cars. I rode faster. I rode past men riding on motorbikes. I rode faster. I rode past women driving in cars. I rode faster. I rode past women riding on motorbikes. I rode faster. I rode past cars. I rode faster. I rode past motorbikes. I rode faster. I rode past men walking on the street. I rode faster. I rode past women walking on the street. I rode faster. I rode past police officers. I rode past Georgia police officers. I rode past officers walking on the street. I rode faster. I rode past police men. I rode past police men driving in police cars. I rode faster. I rode past police men. I rode past police men riding on police motorbikes. I rode faster. I rode past police women. I rode past police women driving in police cars. I rode faster. I rode past police women. I rode past police women riding on police motorbikes. I rode faster. I rode past train stations. I rode past Georgia train stations. I rode farther. I came across somewhere. I came across a police station. I came across Georgia police station. I parked my police motorbike. I parked it in front of the police station. I grabbed my machine gun. I jumped off my motorbike. I walked. I walked forward. I walked towards the police station. I stood in front of the police station. I stood in front of Georgia police station. I stood in front of a giant gate. I looked at the giant gate. I saw the giant gate. I saw it locked. I rolled my eyes. I rolled my blue eyes. I saw something. I saw something happening. I saw something. I saw something strange. I saw something. I saw something strange happening. I saw the giant gate. I saw it opening. I saw it opening faster. I saw it opening faster like a warrior. I saw it opened. I walked. I walked inside the police station. I saw the giant gate. I saw it closing. I saw it closing faster. I saw it closed. I walked. I walked inside the police station. I walked inside Georgia police station. I walked farther. I came across a male police officer. I saw him walking. I saw him walking forward. I saw him walking towards me. I grabbed my giant gun. I pointed it at the male police officer. I shot the male police officer. I shot him one time. I shot him two times. I shot him three times. I shot him multiple times. I saw the male police officer. I saw nothing. I saw nothing happening. I saw nothing. I saw nothing happening to him. I saw the male officer. I saw him walking. I saw him walking forward. I saw him walking towards me. I saw him in front of me. I saw him looking at me. I saw him rolling his eyes. I saw him rolling his green eyes. I saw him grabbing me. I saw him grabbing my neck. I saw him grabbing my neck with one hand. I saw him raising me. I saw him raising me upwards. I saw him raising me above the sky. I saw him holding me. I saw him holding me with one hand. I saw him holding my neck. I saw him holding my neck with one hand. I saw him holding my neck above the sky. I saw him looking at me. I saw him smiling. I saw him smiling at me. I saw him throwing me. I saw him throwing me backwards. I was flying backwards. I was flying farther. I smashed on a heavenly wall. I smashed on a police wall. I dropped on the ground. I dropped on a police ground. I saw nothing. I saw nothing happening to me. I grabbed myself up. I stood up. I looked downwards. I saw my machine gun. I grabbed my machine gun. I grabbed it. I grabbed it with one hand. I was holding my machine gun. I walked. I walked forward. I walked towards the male police officer. I pointed my giant gun. I pointed it forward. I pointed it at the male police officer. I shot the male police officer. I shot him one time. I shot him two times. I shot him three times. I shot him multiple times. I saw the male police officer. I saw him dropping. I saw him dropped on the ground. I saw him dropped on a police ground. I saw him lying on the ground. I saw him lying on a police ground. I saw him lying on a blood-filled ground. I saw him bleeding. I saw his blood on the ground. I saw his blood on a police ground. I saw him dying. I saw him in heavy pain. I saw him breathless. I saw him not breathing. I saw him motionless. I saw him not shaking. I saw him not moving. I saw him dead. I saw him dead on the ground. I saw him dead on a blood-filled ground. I saw him dead on a police ground. I turned around. I walked. I walked farther. I saw a lot of male officers. I saw them walking. I saw them walking towards me. I saw them holding guns. I saw them holding giant guns. I saw them pointing their guns. I saw them pointing their guns at me. I saw them shooting. I saw them walking and shooting. I saw them shooting me. I saw them shooting me one time. I saw them shooting me two times. I saw them shooting me three times. I saw them shooting me four times. I saw them shooting me five times. I saw them shooting me six times. I saw them shooting me seven times. I saw them shooting me eight times. I saw them shooting me nine times. I saw them shooting me ten times. I saw them shooting me multiple times. I saw nothing. I saw nothing happening. I saw nothing. I saw nothing happening to me. I pulled out my machine gun. I pointed it forward. I pointed it at the male police officers. I shot the male police officers. I shot them one time. I shot them two times. I shot them three times. I shot them four times. I shot them five times. I shot them six times. I shot them seven times. I shot them eight times. I shot them nine times. I shot them ten times. I shot them multiple times. I saw all the male police officers. I saw them dropping. I saw them dropped on the ground. I saw them dropped on a police ground. I saw them lying on the ground. I saw them lying on a police ground. I saw them bleeding. I saw their blood. I saw their blood on the ground. I saw their blood on a blood-filled ground. I saw their blood on a police ground. I saw all the male police officers. I saw them dying. I saw them breathless. I saw them not breathing. I saw them motionless. I saw them not shaking. I saw them not moving. I saw them dead. I saw them dead on the ground. I saw them dead on a blood-filled ground. I saw them dead on a police ground. I walked. I walked forward. I walked farther. I saw female police officers. I saw them farther. I saw them walking. I saw them walking farther. I saw them walking towards me. I saw them pulling out their giant guns. I saw them holding their giant guns. I saw them pointing their guns. I saw them pointing their guns at me. I saw them shooting. I saw them walking and shooting. I saw them shooting me. I saw them shooting me one time. I saw them shooting me two times. I saw them shooting me three times. I saw them shooting me four times. I saw them shooting me five times. I saw them shooting me six times. I saw them shooting me seven times. I saw them shooting me eight times. I saw them shooting me nine times. I saw them shooting me ten times. I saw them shooting me multiple times. I saw nothing. I saw nothing happening. I saw nothing. I saw nothing happening to me. I grabbed my giant gun. I pointed it at the female police officers. I shot all the female police officers. I shot them one time. I shot them two times. I shot them three times. I shot them four times. I shot them five times. I shot them six times. I shot them seven times. I shot them eight times. I shot them nine times. I shot them ten times. I shot them multiple times. I saw all the female police officers. I saw all of them dropping. I saw them dropped. I saw them dropped on the ground. I saw them dropped on a police ground. I saw them lying on the ground. I saw them lying on a police ground. I saw them bleeding. I saw their blood on the ground. I saw their blood on a blood-filled ground. I saw their blood on a police ground. I saw them dying. I saw them breathless. I saw them not breathing. I saw them motionless. I saw them not shaking. I saw them not moving. I saw all the female police officers. I saw them dead. I saw them dead on the ground. I saw them dead on a blood-filled ground. I saw them dead on a police ground. I walked. I walked farther. I walked outside the police station. I walked outside Georgia police station. I stood outside the police station. I rolled my eyes. I rolled my blue eyes. I looked farther. I saw someone. I saw someone heavenly. I saw a Lion. I saw him walking. I saw a Lion. I saw him walking farther. I saw a Lion. I saw him walking forward. I saw a Lion. I saw him walking towards me. I saw a Lion. I saw him in front of me. I saw a Lion. I saw him looking at me. I saw a Lion. I saw him speaking. I saw him speaking to me. I saw a Lion. I saw him saying something. I saw him saying something to me. I saw him welcoming Peter Erickson. I saw him welcoming the New York police officer. I saw him welcoming me. I saw him welcoming me to Georgia. I saw him welcoming me to Georgia police station. I saw the Lion. I saw him telling me something. I saw him telling me never to do something. I saw him telling me never to shoot a police officer. I saw the Lion. I saw him speaking out words of wisdom. I saw him speaking out words of freedom. I listened to the Lion. I agreed to his commands. I agreed never to shoot a police officer. I saw the Lion. I saw him doing something. I saw him doing something strange. I saw the Lion. I saw him vanishing. I saw him vanished. I saw him vanished in front of me. I saw the Lion. I saw him no more. I walked. I walked forward. I walked towards my police motorbike. I stood in front of my motorbike. I jumped on my motorbike. I sat on my police motorbike. I grabbed my machine gun. I pushed my hand downwards. I placed my machine gun. I placed it inside my pocket. I pushed my hands forward. I grabbed my motorbike. I pushed my feet downwards. I sparked my motorbike. I sparked it one time. I sparked it two times. I sparked it three times. I sparked it multiple times. I rode on my police motorbike. I rode with my head downwards. I rode faster. I rode past Georgia police station. I rode faster. I turned around. I looked backwards. I saw police cars. I saw police cars chasing me. I saw police motorbikes. I saw police motorbikes chasing me. I saw male police officers. I saw female police officers. I saw Georgia police officers. I saw them driving in police cars. I saw them riding on police motorbikes. I saw them driving faster. I saw them riding faster. I saw them pulling out their guns. I saw them holding their guns. I saw them holding giant guns. I saw them pointing their guns. I saw them pointing their guns at me. I saw them shooting me. I saw them shooting me one time. I saw them shooting me two times. I saw them shooting me three times. I saw them shooting me four times. I saw them shooting me five times. I saw them shooting me six times. I saw them shooting me seven times. I saw them shooting me eight times. I saw them shooting me nine times. I saw them shooting me ten times. I saw them shooting me multiple times. I grabbed my machine gun. I pointed it at the male and female officers. I shot the male and female officers. I shot them on their motorbikes. I shot their police motorbikes. I shot their police cars. I saw their police cars. I saw their police motorbikes. I saw them rolling. I saw them rolling backwards. I saw them rolling farther. I saw them smashing. I saw them smashed on the ground. I saw them smashed on a road. I saw male and female police officers. I saw them dropping. I saw them dropped from their motorbikes. I saw them smashed on the ground. I saw them dropped on a road. I saw them dying. I saw them breathless. I saw them not breathing. I saw them motionless. I saw them not shaking. I saw them not moving. I saw them lifeless. I saw them dead. I saw them dead on the ground. I saw them dead on a road. I saw their police cars. I saw their police motorbikes. I saw them blasting. I saw them blasted. I saw them busting. I saw them busted. I saw them bombing. I saw them bombed. I saw them burning. I saw them burned. I saw them burned on a road. I turned around. I grabbed my police motorbike. I rode on my motorbike. I rode with my head downwards. I rode faster. I rode past the dead police officers. I rode past the burned police cars. I rode past the burned police motorbikes. I rode farther. I came across somewhere. I came across a prison. I came across a prison in Georgia. I parked my police motorbike. I parked it in front of the prison. I grabbed my machine gun. I jumped off my motorbike. I walked. I walked forward. I walked towards the prison. I stood in front of the prison. I stood in front of a giant gate. I looked at the giant gate. I saw the giant gate. I saw it closed. I rolled my eyes. I rolled my blue eyes. I saw something. I saw something happening. I saw something. I saw something strange. I saw something. I saw something strange happening. I saw the prison gate. I saw the giant gate. I saw it opening. I saw it opening faster. I saw it opened. I walked. I walked inside the prison. I saw the giant gate. I saw it closing. I saw it closing faster. I saw it closed. I walked forward. I walked farther. I saw a male prison officer. I saw him walking. I saw him walking forward. I saw him walking towards me. I pulled out my machine gun. I grabbed my giant gun. I walked. I walked forward. I walked towards the male prison officer. I pointed my machine gun. I pointed it at the male prison officer. I shot the male prison officer. I shot him one time. I shot him two times. I shot him three times. I shot him multiple times. I saw the male prison officer. I saw him dropping. I saw him dropped on the ground. I saw him dropped on a prison ground. I saw him bleeding. I saw his blood on the ground. I saw his blood on a blood-filled ground. I saw his blood on a prison ground. I saw him dying. I saw him breathless. I saw him not breathing. I saw him motionless. I saw him not shaking. I saw him not moving. I saw him lifeless. I saw him dead. I saw him dead on the ground. I saw him dead on a blood-filled ground. I saw him dead on a prison ground. I walked. I walked forward. I walked towards the dead prison officer. I stood in front of the dead prison officer. I looked at him. I pushed my hands downwards. I searched him. I searched his pocket. I placed my hands inside his pocket. I pulled out something. I pulled out the prison keys. I pulled out the cells' keys. I grabbed the prison keys. I grabbed the cells' keys. I walked. I walked farther. I saw male prison officers. I saw female prison officers. I saw them walking. I saw them walking forward. I saw them walking towards me. I saw them pulling out guns. I saw them pulling out giant guns. I saw them pointing their guns. I saw them pointing their guns at me. I saw them shooting. I saw them walking and shooting. I saw them shooting me. I saw them shooting me one time. I saw them shooting me two times. I saw them shooting me three times. I saw them shooting me four times. I saw them shooting me five times. I saw them shooting me six times. I saw them shooting me seven times. I saw them shooting me eight times. I saw them shooting me nine times. I saw them shooting me ten times. I saw them shooting me multiple times. I saw nothing. I saw nothing happening. I saw nothing. I saw nothing happening to me. I pulled out my machine gun. I pointed it at the male and female prison officers. I shot the male and female prison officers. I shot them one time. I shot them two times. I shot them three times. I shot them four times. I shot them five times. I shot them six times. I shot them seven times. I shot them eight times. I shot them nine times. I shot them ten times. I shot them multiple times. I saw all the male prison officers. I saw all the female prison officers. I saw them dropping. I saw them dropped on the ground. I saw them dropped on a prison ground. I saw them lying on the ground. I saw them lying on a prison ground. I saw them bleeding. I saw their blood. I saw their blood on the ground. I saw their blood on a blood-filled ground. I saw their blood on a prison ground. I saw them dying. I saw them breathless. I saw them not breathing. I saw them motionless. I saw them not shaking. I saw them not moving. I saw them dead. I saw them dead on the ground. I saw them dead on a prison ground. I saw them dead on a blood-filled ground. I walked forward. I walked farther. I opened all the prison gates. I opened all the cell doors. I freed all the Georgia prisoners. I gave all the Georgia prisoners freedom. I gave freedom to all the Georgia prisoners. I spoke to all the prisoners. I told all of them to wait outside the prison. I told all of them to wait outside for me. I saw all the Georgia prisoners. I saw all of them running. I saw all of them running outside. I saw all of them outside. I saw all of them outside the prison. I saw all of them waiting. I saw all of them waiting for me. I walked. I walked farther. I walked outside the prison. I stood outside Georgia prison. I stood in front of the prisoners. I walked. I walked forward. I walked past the prisoners. I looked forward. I rolled my eyes. I rolled my blue eyes. I saw something. I saw something strange. I saw something. I saw something strange happening. I saw the appearance of motorbikes. I saw hundred police motorbikes. I saw them in front of me. I turned around. I faced the prisoners. I looked at the prisoners. I saw the freed prisoners. I saw them looking at me. I saw them speaking. I saw them speaking to me. I saw them thanking me. I saw them giving me thanksgiving. I saw them thanking me for their freedom. I looked at the freed prisoners. I spoke to them. I told them to jump on the police motorbikes. I told them to jump on the hundred motorbikes. I told them to ride on the hundred motorbikes. I told them to ride back home. I looked at the free prisoners. I saw them looking at me. I saw them speaking. I saw them speaking to me. I saw them saying goodbye. I saw them saying goodbye to Peter Erickson. I saw them saying goodbye to the New York police officer. I saw them saying goodbye to me. I saw them saluting me. I saw them walking. I saw them walking forward. I saw them walking towards the police motorbikes. I saw the Georgia prisoners. I saw them in front of a hundred motorbikes. I saw them jumping on the police motorbikes. I saw them sitting on a hundred motorbikes. I saw them pushing their hands forward. I saw them grabbing their motorbikes. I saw them pushing their feet downwards. I saw them pushing harder. I saw them sparking their motorbikes. I saw them sparking one time. I saw them sparking two times. I saw them sparking three times. I saw them sparking multiple times. I saw the freed prisoners. I saw them riding. I saw them riding on the police motorbikes. I saw them riding on a hundred motorbikes. I saw them riding faster. I saw them riding past me. I saw them riding faster. I saw them riding past Georgia prison. I saw them riding faster. I saw them riding past police cars. I saw them riding faster. I saw them riding past police motorbikes. I saw them riding faster. I saw them riding past train stations. I saw them riding faster. I saw them riding past police stations. I saw them riding farther. I saw them riding back home. I turned around. I looked forward. I saw my police motorbike. I walked. I walked forward. I walked towards my motorbike. I stood in front of my motorbike. I jumped on my motorbike. I sat on my motorbike. I grabbed my machine gun. I pushed it inside my pocket. I pushed my hands forward. I grabbed my motorbike. I pushed my feet downwards. I pushed harder. I sparked my motorbike. I sparked it one time. I sparked it two times. I sparked it three times. I sparked it multiple times. I rode on my police motorbike. I rode with my head downwards. I rode forward. I rode faster. I rode past Georgia prison. I rode faster. I rode past police cars. I rode faster. I rode past police motorbikes. I rode faster. I rode past Georgia train stations. I rode faster. I rode past Georgia police stations. I rode farther. I came across somewhere. I came across another State. I came across another East coast state.

7

THE ASSASSINATION MAN's JOURNEY

FROM

GEORGIA TO VIRGINIA

I rode on my police motorbike. I rode with my head downwards. I rode faster. I rode in Virginia. I rode faster. I rode past cars. I rode faster. I rode past motorbikes. I rode faster. I rode past police cars. I rode faster. I rode past police motorbikes. I rode faster. I rode past train stations. I rode faster. I rode past police officers riding on motorbikes. I rode faster. I rode past police officers driving in cars. I rode faster. I rode past police officers riding on police motorbikes. I rode faster. I rode past police officers driving in police cars. I rode farther. I came across a prison. I came across a prison in Virginia. I parked my police motorbike. I parked it in front of the prison. I pushed my hand inside my pocket. I pulled out my machine gun. I grabbed my machine gun. I jumped off my police motorbike. I walked. I walked forward. I walked towards the prison. I stood in front of the prison. I stood in front of the prison gate. I stood in front of a giant gate. I looked at the giant gate. I saw the giant gate. I saw it closed. I rolled my eyes. I rolled my blue eyes. I saw something. I saw something happening. I saw something. I saw something strange. I saw something. I saw something strange happening. I saw the prison gate. I saw the giant gate. I saw it opening. I saw it opening faster. I saw it opening like a warrior. I saw it opened. I walked. I walked inside the prison. I saw the prison gate. I saw the giant gate. I saw it closing. I saw it closing faster. I saw it closing like a warrior. I saw it closed. I walked. I walked inside the prison. I walked farther. I saw a male prison officer. I saw him walking. I saw him walking forward. I saw him walking towards me. I pulled out my machine gun. I grabbed my giant gun. I pointed it at the male prison officer. I shot the male prison officer. I shot him one time. I shot him two times. I shot him three times. I shot him multiple times. I saw nothing. I saw nothing happening. I saw nothing. I saw nothing happening to him. I saw the male prison officer. I saw him pulling out his gun. I saw him holding a giant gun. I saw him walking. I saw him walking forward. I saw him walking towards me. I saw him pointing his gun. I saw him pointing it at me. I saw him shooting. I saw him walking. I saw him walking and shooting. I saw him shooting me. I saw him shooting me one time. I saw him shooting me two times. I saw him shooting me three times. I saw him shooting me multiple times. I saw nothing. I saw nothing happening. I saw nothing. I saw nothing happening to me. I saw the male prison officer. I saw him in front of me. I pushed my hand forward. I grabbed his neck.

I grabbed his neck with one hand. I raised him upwards. I raised him above the sky. I raised him above the prison sky. I raised him with one hand. I was holding the male prison officer. I was holding him with one hand. I looked at him. I smiled. I smiled at him. I rolled my eyes. I rolled my blue eyes. I threw the male prison officer. I threw him forward. I saw the male prison officer. I saw him smashing. I saw him smashed against a wall. I saw him smashed against a heavenly wall. I saw him smashed against a prison wall. I saw him dropping. I saw him dropped on the ground. I saw him dropped on a prison ground. I saw him lying on the ground. I saw him lying on a prison ground. I saw him dying. I saw him bleeding. I saw his blood. I saw his blood on the ground. I saw his blood on a blood-filled ground. I saw his blood on a prison ground. I saw him dying. I saw him breathless. I saw him not breathing. I saw him motionless. I saw him not shaking. I saw him not moving. I saw the male prison officer. I saw him lifeless. I saw him dead. I saw him dead on the ground. I saw him dead on a blood-filled ground. I saw him dead on a prison ground. I walked. I walked forward. I walked farther. I walked towards the male prison officer. I walked towards a dead prison officer. I stood in front of the dead prison officer. I pushed my hands downwards. I searched the dead prison officer. I searched him. I searched his pockets. I placed my hands inside his pockets. I pulled out something. I pulled out the prison keys. I pulled out the gates' keys. I pulled out the cells' keys. I grabbed the prison keys. I grabbed the gates' keys. I grabbed the cells' keys. I walked. I walked forward. I walked past the dead prison officer. I walked farther. I saw all the male prison officers. I saw them walking. I saw them walking forward. I saw them walking towards me. I saw them pulling out their guns. I saw them holding their guns. I saw them holding giant guns. I saw them pointing their guns. I saw them pointing their guns at me. I saw them shooting. I saw them walking. I saw them walking and shooting. I saw them shooting me. I saw them shooting me one time. I saw them shooting me two times. I saw them shooting me three times. I saw them shooting me four times. I saw them shooting me five times. I saw them shooting me six times. I saw them shooting me seven times. I saw them shooting me eight times. I saw them shooting me nine times. I saw them shooting me ten times. I saw them shooting me multiple times. I saw nothing. I saw nothing happening. I saw nothing. I saw nothing happening to me. I pulled out my machine gun. I grabbed my giant gun. I pointed it at the male prison officers. I shot all the male prison officers. I shot them one time. I shot them two times. I shot them three times. I shot them four times. I shot them five times. I shot them six times. I shot them seven times. I shot them eight times. I shot them nine times. I shot them ten times. I shot them multiple times. I saw all the male prison officers. I saw them dropping. I saw them dropped on the ground. I saw them dropped on a prison ground. I saw them bleeding. I saw their blood. I saw their blood on the ground. I saw their blood on a prison ground. I saw their blood on a blood-filled ground. I saw all the male prison officers. I saw them lying on the ground. I saw them lying on a prison ground. I saw them lying on a blood-filled ground. I saw them dying. I saw them breathless. I saw them not breathing. I saw them motionless. I saw them not shaking. I saw them not moving. I saw them lifeless. I saw them dead. I saw them dead on the ground. I saw them dead on a prison ground. I saw them dead on a blood-filled ground. I walked. I walked forward. I walked past all the dead male prison officers. I walked. I walked farther. I saw all the female prison officers. I saw them running. I saw them running faster. I saw them running forward. I saw them running towards me. I saw them pulling out their guns. I saw them pulling out giant guns. I saw them holding guns. I saw them holding giant guns. I saw them pointing their guns. I saw them pointing their guns at me. I saw them shooting. I saw them running. I saw them running and shooting. I saw them shooting me. I saw them shooting me one time. I saw them shooting me two times. I saw them shooting me three times. I saw them shooting me four times. I saw them shooting me five times. I saw them shooting me six times. I saw them shooting me seven times. I saw them shooting me eight times. I saw them shooting me nine times. I saw them shooting me ten times. I saw them shooting me multiple times. I saw nothing. I saw nothing happening. I saw nothing. I saw nothing happening to me. I pulled out my giant gun. I grabbed my giant gun. I pointed it at the female prison officers. I shot all the female prison officers. I shot them one time. I shot them two times. I shot them three times. I shot them four times. I shot them five times. I shot them six times. I shot them seven times. I shot them eight times. I shot them nine times. I shot them ten times. I shot them multiple times. I saw all the female prison officers. I saw them dropping. I saw them dropped on the ground. I saw them dropped on a prison ground. I saw them lying on the ground. I saw them lying on a prison ground. I saw them bleeding. I saw their blood. I saw their blood on the ground. I saw their blood on a blood-filled ground. I saw their blood on a prison ground. I saw them dying. I saw them breathless. I saw them not breathing. I saw them lifeless. I saw them motionless. I saw them not shaking. I saw them not moving. I saw them dead. I saw them dead on the ground. I saw them dead on a prison ground. I saw them dead on a blood-filled ground. I walked. I walked forward. I walked past all the dead female prison officers. I walked past all the dead prison officers. I walked farther. I opened all the prison gates. I opened all the cell doors. I freed all the prisoners. I gave all the prisoners freedom. I spoke to all the freed prisoners. I told them to run outside. I told them to wait outside. I told them to wait outside the prison. I told them to wait for me. I saw all the freed prisoners. I saw them running. I saw them running outside. I saw them outside the prison. I saw them waiting. I saw them waiting outside. I saw them waiting for me. I walked. I walked outside the prison. I walked. I walked forward. I walked past the freed prisoners. I stood in front of the freed prisoners. I looked forward. I rolled my eyes. I rolled my blue eyes. I saw something. I saw something strange. I saw something. I saw something strange happening. I saw hundreds of police motorbikes. I saw them appearing. I saw them appeared. I saw them appeared in front of me. I saw hundreds of motorbikes. I saw them in front of me. I turned around. I faced the freed prisoners. I spoke to all the freed prisoners. I told them to jump on the police motorbikes. I told them to ride on the police motorbikes. I told them to ride faster. I told them to ride back home. I looked at the freed prisoners. I saw the freed prisoners. I saw them looking at me. I saw them speaking. I saw them speaking to me. I saw them thanking Peter Erickson. I saw them thanking the New York police officer. I saw them thanking me. I saw them giving me thanksgiving. I saw them thanking me for their freedom. I saw all the freed prisoners. I saw them saying goodbye. I saw them saying goodbye to Peter Erickson. I saw them saying goodbye to the New York police officer. I saw them saying goodbye to me. I saw all the freed Virginia prisoners. I saw all the freed prisoners. I saw them walking. I saw them walking forward. I saw them walking past me. I saw them walking towards a hundred motorbikes. I saw them in front of a hundred motorbikes. I saw them jumping on the motorbikes. I saw them sitting on the police motorbikes. I saw them pushing their hands forward. I saw them grabbing the motorbikes. I saw them pushing their feet downwards. I saw them pushing harder. I saw them sparking the motorbikes. I saw them sparking one time. I saw them sparking two times. I saw them sparking three times. I saw them sparking multiple times. I saw them riding. I saw them riding on hundreds of motorbikes. I saw them riding with their head downwards. I saw them riding forward. I saw them riding faster. I saw them riding past me. I saw them riding faster. I saw them riding past Virginia prison. I saw them riding faster. I saw them riding past cars. I saw them riding faster. I saw them riding past motorbikes. I saw them riding faster. I saw them riding past police cars. I saw them riding faster. I saw them riding past police motorbikes. I saw them riding faster. I saw them riding past police stations. I saw them riding faster. I saw them riding past Virginia train stations. I saw them riding farther. I saw them riding back home. I walked. I walked forward. I walked towards my police motorbike. I stood in front of my motorbike. I jumped on my motorbike. I sat on my motorbike. I grabbed my machine gun. I grabbed my giant gun. I pushed my hands downwards. I pushed my machine gun. I pushed the giant gun. I pushed them inside my pockets. I pushed my hands forward. I grabbed my police motorbike. I pushed my feet downwards. I pushed harder. I sparked my motorbike. I sparked it one time. I sparked it two times. I sparked it three times. I sparked it multiple times. I rode on my police motorbike. I rode with my head downwards. I rode faster. I rode past Virginia prison. I rode faster. I rode past cars. I rode faster. I rode past motorbikes. I rode faster. I rode past police cars. I rode faster. I rode past police motorbikes. I rode faster. I turned around. I looked backwards. I saw police cars. I saw police cars chasing me. I saw Virginia police officers. I saw them driving in police cars. I saw them pulling out their guns. I saw them holding giant guns. I saw their heads outside the car windows. I saw them pointing their giant guns. I saw them pointing their guns at me. I saw them shooting. I saw them driving. I saw them driving and shooting. I saw them shooting me. I saw nothing. I saw nothing happening. I saw nothing. I saw nothing happening to me. I pulled out my machine gun. I grabbed my machine gun. I pointed it at the police cars. I shot the police cars. I shot the police cars one time. I shot the police cars two times. I shot the police cars three times. I shot the police cars multiple times. I saw something. I saw something happening. I saw the police cars. I saw them rolling. I saw them rolling on the road. I saw them rolling backwards. I saw them smashing. I saw them smashed. I saw them smashed on the road. I saw them dropping. I saw them dropped. I saw them dropped on the road. I saw the police cars. I saw them blasting. I saw them blasted. I saw them busting. I saw them busted. I saw them bombing. I saw them bombed. I saw them burning. I saw them burned. I rode on my police motorbike. I rode with my head downwards. I rode faster. I rode past burning police cars. I rode faster. I rode past burned police cars. I rode faster. I looked backwards. I saw police officers. I saw Virginia police officers. I saw them riding. I saw them riding on police motorbikes. I saw them riding faster. I saw them chasing me. I saw them pulling out giant guns. I saw them holding giant guns. I saw them pointing their guns. I saw them pointing their guns at me. I saw them riding. I saw them riding on their motorbikes. I saw them shooting. I saw them riding and shooting. I saw them shooting me. I saw them shooting me one time. I saw them shooting me two times. I saw them shooting me three times. I saw them shooting me four times. I saw them shooting me five times. I saw them shooting me six times. I saw them shooting me seven times. I saw them shooting me eight times. I saw them shooting me nine times. I saw them shooting me ten times. I saw them shooting me multiple times. I saw nothing. I saw nothing happening. I saw nothing. I saw nothing happening to me. I pulled out my machine gun. I grabbed my machine gun. I pointed it at the police motorbikes. I shot the police motorbikes. I shot the police officers. I shot them one time. I shot them two times. I shot them three times. I shot them four times. I shot them five times. I shot them six times. I shot them seven times. I shot them eight times. I shot them nine times. I shot them ten times. I shot them multiple times. I saw the police motorbikes. I saw the police officers. I saw them smashing. I saw them smashed. I saw them smashed on the road. I saw them dropping. I saw them dropped. I saw them dropped on the road. I saw the police motorbikes. I saw them rolling. I saw them rolling backwards. I saw them rolling on the road. I saw them blasting. I saw them blasted. I saw them busting. I saw them busted. I saw them bombing. I saw them bombed. I saw them burning. I saw them burned. I saw the Virginia police officers. I saw them rolling. I saw them rolling backwards. I saw them smashing. I saw them smashed. I saw them smashed on the road. I saw them dropping. I saw them dropped. I saw them dropped on the road. I saw them lying on the road. I saw them breathless. I saw them not breathing. I saw them dying. I saw them motionless. I saw them not shaking. I saw them not moving. I saw them dead. I saw them dead on the road. I rode on my police motorbike. I rode with my head downwards. I rode faster. I rode past burning motorbikes. I rode faster. I rode past burned motorbikes. I rode faster. I rode past dead police officers. I rode faster. I rode past Virginia prisons. I rode faster. I rode past Virginia police stations. I rode faster. I rode past cars. I rode faster. I rode past motorbikes. I rode faster. I rode past police cars. I rode faster. I rode past police motorbikes. I rode faster. I rode past Virginia train stations. I rode farther. I came across somewhere. I came across another state. I came across another East coast state.

8

THE ASSASSINATION MAN's JOURNEY

FROM VIRGINIA TO MARYLAND

I rode on my police motorbike. I rode with my head downwards. I rode faster. I rode in Maryland. I rode faster. I rode past police cars. I rode faster. I rode past police motorbikes. I rode faster. I rode past police stations. I rode faster. I rode past train stations. I rode faster. I rode past prisons. I rode faster. I rode past police officers driving in police cars. I rode faster. I rode past police officers riding on police motorbikes. I rode farther. I came across somewhere. I came across a prison. I came across a prison in Maryland. I parked my police motorbike. I parked it in front of the prison. I pushed my hands downwards. I pushed my hands inside my pockets. I pulled out my giant guns. I grabbed my two guns. I jumped off my police motorbike. I walked. I walked forward. I walked towards the prison. I stood in front of the prison. I stood in front of a giant gate. I looked at the giant gate. I saw the giant gate. I saw it closed. I rolled my eyes. I rolled my blue eyes. I saw something. I saw something strange. I saw something. I saw something strange happening. I saw the prison gate. I saw the giant gate. I saw it opening. I saw it opening faster. I saw it opened. I walked. I walked inside the prison. I saw the prison gate. I saw the giant gate. I saw it closing. I saw it closing like a warrior. I saw it closing faster. I saw it closing faster than a warrior. I saw it closed. I walked. I walked forward. I walked farther. I saw one female prison officer. I saw her walking. I saw her walking forward. I saw her walking towards me. I pulled out my giant gun. I grabbed my giant gun. I pointed it at the female prison officer. I shot the female prison officer. I shot her. I shot her one time. I shot her two times. I shot her three times. I shot her multiple times. I saw the female prison officer. I saw nothing. I saw nothing happening. I saw nothing. I saw nothing happening to her. I saw her. I saw her pulling out her gun. I saw her pulling out a giant gun. I saw her. I saw her grabbing her gun. I saw her grabbing a giant gun. I saw her pointing the giant gun. I saw her pointing it at me. I saw her shooting. I saw her walking. I saw her walking towards me. I saw her walking. I saw her walking and shooting. I saw her shooting me. I saw her shooting me one time. I saw her shooting me two times. I saw her shooting me three times. I saw her shooting me multiple times. I saw nothing. I saw nothing happening. I saw nothing. I saw nothing happening to me. I saw the female prison officer. I saw her. I saw her in front of me. I looked at her. I rolled my eyes. I rolled my blue eyes. I pushed my hand forward. I grabbed her. I grabbed her with one hand. I grabbed her neck. I grabbed her neck with one hand. I raised her. I raised her with one hand. I raised her upwards. I raised her above the sky. I raised her above the prison sky. I was holding her. I was holding her with one hand. I looked at her. I smiled. I smiled at her. I rolled my eyes. I rolled my blue eyes. I threw her. I threw her forward. I saw her. I saw her farther. I saw her flying. I saw her flying backwards. I saw her smashing. I saw her smashed on a wall. I saw her smashed on a heavenly wall. I saw her smashed on a prison wall. I saw her dropping. I saw her dropped. I saw her dropped on the ground. I saw her dropped on a prison ground. I saw her farther. I saw her lying on the ground. I saw her lying on a prison ground. I saw her lying on a blood-filled ground. I saw her dying. I saw her bleeding. I saw her blood. I saw her blood on the ground. I saw her blood on a prison ground. I saw her blood on a blood-filled ground. I saw her dying. I saw her breathless. I saw her not breathing. I saw her in heavy pain. I saw her motionless. I saw her not shaking. I saw her not moving. I saw the female prison officer. I saw her dead. I saw her dead on the ground. I saw her dead on a prison ground. I saw her dead on a blood-filled ground. I walked. I walked forward. I walked. I walked towards the dead female prison officer. I walked farther. I stood in front of her. I pushed my hands downwards. I searched her. I searched her pockets. I searched for the prison keys. I searched for the cells' keys. I pulled out the prison keys. I pulled out the cells' keys. I grabbed the prison keys. I grabbed the cells' keys. I walked. I walked forward. I walked past the dead female prison officer. I walked past her. I walked. I walked farther. I saw female prison officers. I saw them farther. I saw them running. I saw them running towards me. I saw them running faster. I saw them pulling out giant guns. I saw them holding giant guns. I saw them pointing the giant guns. I saw them pointing the giant guns forward. I saw them pointing the giant guns at me. I saw them shooting. I saw them running. I saw them running and shooting. I saw them shooting me. I saw them shooting me one time. I saw them shooting me two times. I saw them shooting me three times. I saw them shooting me four times. I saw them shooting me five times. I saw them shooting me six times. I saw them shooting me seven times. I saw them shooting me eight times. I saw them shooting me nine times. I saw them shooting me ten times. I saw them shooting me multiple times. I saw nothing. I saw nothing happening. I saw nothing. I saw nothing happening to me. I looked at the female prison officers. I rolled my eyes. I rolled my blue eyes. I pulled out my guns. I pulled out my machine gun. I pulled out my giant gun. I grabbed my guns. I grabbed my giant gun. I grabbed my machine gun. I pointed my guns. I pointed my giant gun. I pointed my machine gun. I pointed them at the female prison officers. I shot all the female prison officers. I shot them one time. I shot them two times. I shot them three times. I shot them four times. I shot them five times. I shot them six times. I shot them seven times. I shot them eight times. I shot them nine times. I shot them ten times. I shot them multiple times. I saw all the female prison officers. I saw them dropping. I saw them dropped. I saw them dropped on the ground. I saw them dropped on a prison ground. I saw them lying on the ground. I saw them lying on a prison ground. I saw them bleeding. I saw their blood. I saw their blood on the ground. I saw their blood on a prison ground. I saw their blood on a blood-filled ground. I saw them dying. I saw them breathless. I saw them not breathing. I saw them motionless. I saw them not shaking. I saw them not moving. I saw all the female prison officers. I saw them dead. I saw them dead on the ground. I saw them dead on a prison ground. I saw them dead on a blood-filled ground. I walked. I walked forward. I walked past all the dead female prison officers. I walked farther. I looked farther. I saw a lot of male prison officers. I saw them pulling out giant guns. I saw them holding giant guns. I saw them running. I saw them running forward. I saw them running towards me. I saw them running faster. I saw them grabbing their guns. I saw them grabbing giant guns. I saw them pointing the giant guns. I saw them pointing their guns at me. I saw them shooting. I saw them running. I saw them running towards me. I saw them running and shooting. I saw them shooting me. I saw them shooting me one time. I saw them shooting me two times. I saw them shooting me three times. I saw them shooting me four times. I saw them shooting me five times. I saw them shooting me six times. I saw them shooting me seven times. I saw them shooting me eight times. I saw them shooting me nine times. I saw them shooting me ten times. I saw them shooting me multiple times. I saw nothing. I saw nothing happening. I saw nothing. I saw nothing happening to me. I pulled out my guns. I pulled out my giant guns. I pulled out my giant gun. I pulled out my machine gun. I grabbed my guns. I grabbed my giant guns. I grabbed my giant gun. I grabbed my machine gun. I pointed my two guns. I pointed my giant guns. I pointed my giant gun. I pointed my machine gun. I pointed them forward. I pointed them at the male prison officers. I shot all the male prison officers. I shot all the male Maryland prison officers. I shot them one time. I shot them two times. I shot them three times. I shot them four times. I shot them five times. I shot them six times. I shot them seven times. I shot them eight times. I shot them nine times. I shot them ten times. I shot them multiple times. I saw all the male prison officers. I saw them dropping. I saw them dropped. I saw them dropped on the ground. I saw them dropped on a prison ground. I saw them lying on the ground. I saw them lying on a prison ground. I saw them dying. I saw them bleeding. I saw their blood. I saw their blood on the ground. I saw their blood on a prison ground. I saw their blood on a blood-filled ground. I saw them breathless. I saw them not breathing. I saw a static for a major. I saw them motionless. I saw them not shaking. I saw them not moving. I saw all the male prison officers. I saw them dead. I saw them dead on the ground. I saw them dead on a prison ground. I saw them dead on a blood-filled ground. I walked. I walked forward. I walked past the dead male prison officers. I walked farther. I opened all the prison gates. I opened all the prison cells. I freed all the Maryland prisoners. I gave all the prisoners freedom. I gave freedom to all the prisoners. I spoke to all the prisoners. I told them to walk outside. I told them to walk outside the prison. I told them to wait outside. I told them to wait outside the prison. I told them to wait for me. I saw all the Maryland prisoners. I saw all the freed prisoners. I saw all the freedom prisoners. I saw them walking. I saw them walking outside. I saw them outside. I saw them outside the prison. I saw them waiting. I saw them waiting outside the prison. I saw them waiting for me. I walked. I walked farther. I walked outside the prison. I walked. I walked forward. I walked past the Maryland prisoners. I walked past all the prisoners. I stood in front of the freed prisoners. I looked forward. I rolled my eyes. I rolled my blue eyes. I saw something. I saw something appearing. I saw the appearance of motorbikes. I saw hundreds of police motorbikes. I saw them appearing. I saw them appeared. I saw them appeared in front of me. I saw hundreds of police motorbikes. I saw them in front of me. I turned around. I faced the Maryland prisoners. I faced all the freed prisoners. I saw all the freed prisoners. I spoke to all the Maryland prisoners. I spoke to all the freed prisoners. I spoke to all the freed prisoners. I told them to jump on the hundred motorbikes. I told them to jump on the police motorbikes. I told them to ride back home. I looked forward. I looked at all the Maryland prisoners. I saw all the freed prisoners. I saw them looking at me. I saw them speaking. I saw them speaking to me. I saw them thanking me. I saw them giving me thanksgiving. I saw them thanking me for giving them freedom. I saw them downwards. I saw them saluting me. I looked forward. I looked at all the prisoners. I saw all the Maryland prisoners. I saw all the freed prisoners. I saw them speaking. I saw them speaking to me. I saw them saying goodbye. I saw them saying goodbye to Peter Erickson. I saw them saying goodbye to the New York police officer. I saw them saying goodbye to me. I saw them walking. I saw them walking forward. I saw them walking past me. I saw them walking towards hundreds of motorbikes. I saw them in front of a hundred motorbikes. I saw them in front of police motorbikes. I saw them jumping. I saw them jumping on the police motorbikes. I saw them sitting on the police motorbikes. I saw them pushing their hands forward. I saw them grabbing the police motorbikes. I saw them pushing their feet downwards. I saw them pushing harder. I saw them sparking. I saw them sparking the police motorbikes. I saw them sparking one time. I saw them sparking two times. I saw them sparking three times. I saw them sparking multiple times. I saw them riding. I saw them riding on the police motorbikes. I saw them riding on hundreds of motorbikes. I saw them riding forward. I saw them riding faster. I saw them riding past me. I saw them riding faster. I saw them riding past Maryland prison. I saw them riding faster. I saw them riding past police cars. I saw them riding faster. I saw them riding past police motorbikes. I saw them riding faster. I saw them riding past cars. I saw them riding faster. I saw them riding past motorbikes. I saw them riding faster. I saw them riding past police stations. I saw them riding faster. I saw them riding past train stations. I saw them riding farther. I saw them riding back home. I walked. I walked forward. I walked towards my police motorbike. I stood in front of my police motorbike. I jumped. I jumped on my motorbike. I sat on my motorbike. I grabbed my two guns. I grabbed my giant gun. I grabbed my machine gun. I pushed my hands inside my pockets. I pushed my two guns. I pushed them inside my pockets. I pushed my hands forward. I grabbed my motorbike. I pushed my feet downwards. I sparked my motorbike. I sparked it. I sparked it one time. I sparked it two times. I sparked it three times. I sparked it multiple times. I rode on my police motorbike. I rode with my head downwards. I rode forward. I rode faster. I rode past Maryland prison. I rode faster. I turned around. I looked backwards. I saw police cars. I saw police cars chasing me. I saw police motorbikes. I saw police motorbikes chasing me. I saw police officers. I saw Maryland police officers. I saw them driving in police cars. I saw them chasing me. I saw Maryland police officers. I saw them riding on police motorbikes. I saw them chasing me. I pulled out my machine gun. I pointed it at the police cars. I shot all the police cars. I shot them one time. I shot them two times. I shot them three times. I shot them four times. I shot them five times. I shot them six times. I shot them seven times. I shot them eight times. I shot them nine times. I shot them ten times. I shot them multiple times. I saw all the police cars. I saw them rolling. I saw them rolling backwards. I saw them smashing. I saw them smashed. I saw them smashed on the road. I saw them dropping. I saw them dropped. I saw them dropped on the road. I saw the police cars. I saw them blasting. I saw them blasted. I saw them busting. I saw them busted. I saw them bombing. I saw them bombed. I saw them on fire. I saw them burning. I saw them burned. I saw Maryland police officers. I saw them riding. I saw them riding on police motorbikes. I saw them riding forward. I saw them riding faster. I saw them chasing me. I saw them pulling out giant guns. I saw them pointing giant guns. I saw them pointing giant guns at me. I saw them shooting. I saw them riding. I saw them riding and shooting. I saw them shooting me. I saw them shooting me one time. I saw them shooting me two times. I saw them shooting me three times. I saw them shooting me four times. I saw them shooting me five times. I saw them shooting me six times. I saw them shooting me seven times. I saw them shooting me eight times. I saw them shooting me nine times. I saw them shooting me ten times. I saw them shooting me multiple times. I saw nothing. I saw nothing happening. I saw nothing. I saw nothing happening to me. I pulled out my giant gun. I grabbed my giant gun. I grabbed it. I pointed it at police officers. I pointed it at officers riding on motorbikes. I shot all the police officers. I shot them on their police motorbikes. I shot them one time. I shot them two times. I shot them three times. I shot them four times. I shot them five times. I shot them six times. I shot them seven times. I shot them eight times. I shot them nine times. I shot them ten times. I shot them multiple times. I saw all the police officers. I saw them dropping. I saw them dropped. I saw them dropped on the ground. I saw them dropped on a road. I saw them rolling. I saw them rolling on the road. I saw them rolling backwards. I saw them lying. I saw them lying on a road. I saw them dying. I saw them breathless. I saw them not breathing. I saw them motionless. I saw them not shaking. I saw them not moving. I saw a static for a major. I saw them dead. I saw them dead on the ground. I saw them dead on a road. I saw the police motorbikes. I saw them rolling. I saw them rolling on a road. I saw them rolling backwards. I saw them smashing. I saw them smashed. I saw them smashed on a road. I saw them dropping. I saw them dropped. I saw them dropped on a road. I saw them blasting. I saw them blasted. I saw them busting. I saw them busted. I saw them bombing. I saw them bombed. I saw them on fire. I saw them burning. I saw them burned. I turned around. I faced forward. I pushed my giant gun. I pushed it inside my pocket. I pushed my hands forward. I grabbed my police motorbike. I rode on my police motorbike. I rode with my head downwards. I rode faster. I rode past burning police cars. I rode faster. I rode past burned police cars. I rode faster. I rode past burning police motorbikes. I rode faster. I rode past burned police motorbikes. I rode faster. I rode past dead police officers. I rode faster. I rode past police stations. I rode faster. I rode past police cars. I rode faster. I rode past police motorbikes. I rode faster. I rode past officers driving in police cars. I rode faster. I rode past officers riding on police motorbikes. I rode farther. I came across somewhere. I came across another state. I came across another East coast state.

9

THE ASSASSINATION MAN's JOURNEY

FROM

MARYLAND TO NEW JERSEY

I rode on my police motorbike. I rode with my head downwards. I rode faster. I rode inside New Jersey. I rode faster. I rode past police cars. I rode faster. I rode past police motorbikes. I rode faster. I rode past train stations. I rode faster. I rode past police stations. I rode faster. I rode past cars. I rode faster. I rode past motorbikes. I rode farther. I came across somewhere. I came across a prison. I came across a prison in New Jersey. I parked my police motorbike. I parked it in front of the prison. I pushed my hands inside my pockets. I pulled out my two guns. I pulled out my two giant guns. I pulled out my machine guns. I grabbed my machine guns. I jumped. I jumped off my motorbike. I walked. I walked forward. I walked towards the prison. I stood in front of the prison. I stood in front of two giant gates. I looked at the giant gates. I saw the giant gates. I saw them closed. I rolled my eyes. I rolled my blue eyes. I saw the two giant gates. I saw them opening. I saw them opening like a warrior. I saw them opening faster. I saw them opened. I walked. I walked inside the prison. I walked inside New Jersey prison. I walked farther. I saw one female prison officer. I saw her walking. I saw her walking forward. I saw her walking towards me. I grabbed my giant gun. I pointed it. I pointed it forward. I pointed it at the female prison officer. I shot the female prison officer. I shot her. I shot her one time. I shot her two times. I shot her three times. I shot her multiple times. I saw the female prison officer. I saw her. I saw her dropping. I saw her dropped. I saw her dropped on the ground. I saw her dropped on a prison ground. I saw her lying on the ground. I saw her lying on a prison ground. I saw her lying on a blood-filled ground. I saw her bleeding. I saw her blood on the ground. I saw her blood on a prison ground. I saw her blood on a blood-filled ground. I saw her dying. I saw her breathless. I saw her not breathing. I saw her motionless. I saw her not shaking. I saw her not moving. I saw her dead. I saw her dead on the ground. I saw her dead on a prison ground. I saw her dead on a blood-filled ground. I walked. I walked forward. I walked towards the dead female prison officer. I stood in front of her. I pushed my hands downwards. I searched her. I searched her pockets. I searched for the prison keys. I searched for the gate keys. I searched for the cells' keys. I found the prison keys. I found the gate keys. I found the cells' keys. I found them inside her pockets. I grabbed the prison keys. I grabbed the gate keys. I grabbed the cells' keys. I walked. I walked forward. I walked past her. I walked farther. I saw a lot of prison officers. I saw a lot of male prison officers. I saw a lot of female prison officers. I saw them running. I saw them running forward. I saw them running towards me. I saw them pulling out their guns. I saw them pulling out giant guns. I saw them holding giant guns. I saw them shooting. I saw them running and shooting. I saw them shooting me. I saw them shooting me one time. I saw them shooting me two times. I saw them shooting me three times. I saw them shooting me four times. I saw them shooting me five times. I saw them shooting me six times. I saw them shooting me seven times. I saw them shooting me eight times. I saw them shooting me nine times. I saw them shooting me ten times. I saw them shooting me multiple times. I saw nothing. I saw nothing happening. I saw nothing. I saw nothing happening to me. I pulled out my machine gun. I grabbed my machine gun. I pointed it forward. I pointed it at all the prison officers. I pointed it at the male prison officers. I pointed it at the female prison officers. I shot all the prison officers. I shot all the male prison officers. I shot all the female prison officers. I shot them one time. I shot them two times. I shot them three times. I shot them four times. I shot them five times. I shot them six times. I shot them seven times. I shot them eight times. I shot them nine times. I shot them ten times. I shot them multiple times. I saw all the male prison officers. I saw all the female prison officers. I saw them dropping. I saw them dropped. I saw them dropped on the ground. I saw them dropped on a prison ground. I saw them lying on the ground. I saw them lying on a prison ground. I saw them dying. I saw them bleeding. I saw their blood. I saw their blood on the ground. I saw their blood on a prison ground. I saw their blood on a blood-filled ground. I saw them breathless. I saw them not breathing. I saw them motionless. I saw them not shaking. I saw them not moving. I saw them dead. I saw them dead on the ground. I saw them dead on a prison ground. I saw them dead on a blood-filled ground. I walked. I walked forward. I walked past the dead prison officers. I walked. I walked farther. I opened all the prison gates. I opened all the cell doors. I freed all the prisoners. I freed all the prisoners in New Jersey. I gave all the prisoners freedom. I gave freedom to all the New Jersey prisoners. I spoke to all the prisoners. I told them to walk out. I told them to walk outside. I told them to walk outside the prison. I told them to wait outside. I told them to wait outside the prison. I told them to wait for me. I saw all the prisoners. I saw them walking. I saw them walking outside. I saw them outside. I saw them outside the prison. I saw them waiting. I saw them waiting outside. I saw them waiting outside the prison. I saw them waiting for me. I walked. I walked farther. I walked outside. I walked outside the prison. I stood in front of the prisoners. I walked. I walked forward. I looked farther. I rolled my eyes. I rolled my blue eyes. I saw something. I saw something strange. I saw something. I saw something strange happening. I saw hundreds of police motorbikes. I saw them appearing. I saw them appeared. I saw them appeared in front of me. I turned around. I faced the prisoners. I spoke to the prisoners. I told them to jump on the hundred motorbikes. I told them to ride on the police motorbikes. I told them to ride faster. I told them to ride back home. I looked at the freed prisoners. I saw them looking at me.

I saw them speaking. I saw them speaking to me. I saw them thanking me. I saw them giving me thanks. I saw them giving me thanksgiving. I saw them thanking me for giving them freedom. I saw all the freed prisoners. I saw them speaking. I saw them speaking to me. I saw them saying goodbye. I saw them saying goodbye to Peter Erickson. I saw them saying goodbye to the New York police officer. I saw them saying goodbye to me. I saw the freed prisoners. I saw them walking. I saw them walking forward. I saw them walking past me. I saw them walking towards hundreds of motorbikes. I saw them in front of a hundred motorbikes. I saw them in front of police motorbikes. I saw them jumping on the motorbikes. I saw them sitting on the motorbikes. I saw them pushing their hands forward. I saw them grabbing the police motorbikes. I saw them pushing their feet downwards. I saw them pushing harder. I saw them sparking. I saw them sparking the motorbikes. I saw them sparking one time. I saw them sparking two times. I saw them sparking three times. I saw them sparking multiple times. I saw them riding. I saw them riding on the police motorbikes. I saw them riding forward. I saw them riding with their head downwards. I saw them riding faster. I saw them riding past me. I saw them riding past the prison. I saw them riding past New Jersey prison. I saw them riding faster. I saw them riding past New Jersey train stations. I saw them riding faster. I saw them riding past New Jersey police stations. I saw them riding faster. I saw them riding past police cars. I saw them riding faster. I saw them riding past police motorbikes. I saw them riding farther. I saw them riding back home. I walked. I walked forward. I walked towards my police motorbike. I stood in front of my motorbike. I jumped on my motorbike. I sat on my motorbike. I grabbed my giant guns. I grabbed my machine gun. I grabbed my giant gun. I pushed them inside my pockets. I pushed my hands forward. I grabbed my motorbike. I pushed my feet downwards. I pushed harder. I sparked my motorbike. I sparked it. I sparked it one time. I sparked it two times. I sparked it three times. I sparked it multiple times. I rode on my police motorbike. I rode with my head downwards. I rode forward. I rode faster. I rode past New Jersey Prison. I rode faster. I rode past New Jersey train stations. I rode faster. I rode past New Jersey police stations. I rode faster. I rode past police cars. I rode faster. I rode past police motorbikes. I rode faster. I rode past walking officers. I rode faster. I rode past officers driving in police cars. I rode faster. I rode past officers riding on police motorbikes. I rode faster. I turned around. I looked backwards. I saw police cars. I saw police motorbikes. I saw officers driving in police cars. I saw officers riding on police motorbikes. I saw them chasing me. I pulled out my machine gun. I pointed it. I pointed it at the police cars. I shot the police cars. I pointed it at the police motorbikes. I shot the police motorbikes. I shot them one time. I shot them two times. I shot them three times. I shot them four times. I shot them five times. I shot them six times. I shot them seven times. I shot them eight times. I shot them nine times. I shot them ten times. I shot them multiple times. I saw the police cars. I saw the police motorbikes. I saw them flying. I saw them flying backwards. I saw them rolling. I saw them rolling backwards. I saw them rolling on the ground. I saw them rolling on the road. I saw them smashing. I saw them smashed. I saw them smashed on the road. I saw them dropping. I saw them dropped. I saw them dropped on a road. I saw them blasting. I saw them blasted. I saw them blasted on a road. I saw them busting. I saw them busted. I saw them busted on a road. I saw them bombing. I saw them bombed. I saw them bombed on a road. I saw them on fire. I saw them burning. I saw them burned. I saw the police officers. I saw them flying. I saw them flying from their motorbikes. I saw them flying backwards. I saw them flying farther. I saw them flying like warriors. I saw them dropping. I saw them dropped. I saw them dropped on a road. I saw them lying on a road. I saw them dying. I saw them breathless. I saw them not breathing. I saw a static for a major. I saw them motionless. I saw them not shaking. I saw them not moving. I saw New Jersey police officers. I saw them dead. I saw them dead on the ground. I saw them dead on a road. I turned around. I faced forward. I pushed my machine gun. I pushed it inside my pockets. I grabbed my motorbike. I rode on my motorbike. I rode forward. I rode faster. I rode past burning police cars. I rode faster. I rode past burned police cars. I rode faster. I rode past burning police motorbikes. I rode faster. I rode past burned police motorbikes. I rode faster. I rode past police cars. I rode faster. I rode past police motorbikes. I rode faster. I rode past police officers. I rode faster. I rode past officers driving in police cars. I rode faster. I rode past officers riding on police motorbikes. I rode farther. I came across somewhere. I came another state. I came across another East coast state.

10

THE ASSASSINATION MAN's JOURNEY

FROM NEW JERSEY TO CONNECTICUT I rode on my police motorbike. I rode with my head downwards. I rode faster. I rode inside Connecticut. I rode faster. I rode past train stations. I rode faster. I rode past police stations. I rode faster. I rode past police cars. I rode faster. I rode past police motorbikes. I rode faster. I rode past walking police officers. I rode faster. I rode past officers. I rode past Connecticut officers. I rode past police officers. I rode past Connecticut police officers. I rode past officers driving police cars. I rode faster. I rode past officers riding on police motorbikes. I rode farther. I came across somewhere. I came across a prison. I came across a prison in Connecticut. I parked my police motorbike. I parked it in front of the prison. I pushed my hand inside my pocket. I grabbed my giant gun. I jumped. I jumped off my motorbike. I walked. I walked forward. I walked towards the prison. I stood in front of the prison. I stood in front of a giant gate. I looked. I looked at the giant gate. I saw the giant gate. I saw it closed. I rolled my eyes. I rolled my blue eyes. I saw something. I saw something happening. I saw something. I saw something strange. I saw something. I saw something strange happening. I saw the prison gate. I saw the giant gate. I saw it opening. I saw it opening like a warrior. I saw it opening faster. I saw it opened. I walked. I walked inside the prison. I walked farther. I saw a male prison officer. I saw him walking. I saw him walking forward. I saw him walking towards me. I pulled out my giant gun. I grabbed it. I pointed it. I pointed it at the male prison officer. I shot him. I shot the male prison officer. I shot him one time. I shot him two times. I shot him three times. I shot him multiple times. I saw the male prison officer. I saw him dropping. I saw him dropped. I saw him dropped on the ground. I saw him dropped on a prison ground. I saw him lying on the ground. I saw him lying on a prison ground. I saw him lying on a blood-filled ground. I saw him dying. I saw his blood. I saw his blood on the ground. I saw his blood on a prison ground. I saw his blood on a blood-filled ground. I saw him dying. I saw him breathless. I saw him not breathing. I saw him motionless. I saw him not shaking. I saw him not moving. I saw him dead. I saw him dead on the ground. I saw him dead on a prison ground. I saw him dead on a blood-filled ground. I walked. I walked forward. I walked towards the dead prison officer. I stood in front of him. I pushed my hands downwards. I pushed my hands inside his pockets. I searched him. I searched for the prison keys. I searched for the cells' keys. I found the prison keys. I found the cells keys. I found them inside his pockets. I pulled out the prison keys. I pulled out the cells' keys. I grabbed the prison keys. I grabbed the cells' keys. I walked. I walked forward. I walked past the dead prison officer. I walked farther. I looked. I looked farther. I saw a lot of male prison officers. I saw a lot of female prison officers. I saw them farther. I saw them running. I saw them running forward. I saw them running towards me. I saw them pulling out their guns. I saw them pulling out giant guns. I saw them holding giant guns. I saw them pointing their guns. I saw them pointing giant guns. I saw them pointing giant guns at me. I saw a lot of male prison officers. I saw a lot of female prison officers. I saw them shooting. I saw them running. I saw them running and shooting. I saw them shooting me. I saw them shooting me one time. I saw them shooting me two times. I saw them shooting me three times. I saw them shooting me four times. I saw them shooting me five times. I saw them shooting me six times. I saw them shooting me seven times. I saw them shooting me eight times. I saw them shooting me nine times. I saw them shooting me ten times. I saw them shooting me multiple times. I saw nothing. I saw nothing happening. I saw nothing. I saw nothing happening to me. I pulled out my giant gun. I grabbed my giant gun. I pointed it. I pointed it at the male prison officers. I pointed it at the female prison officers. I shot all the male prison officers. I shot all the female prison officers. I shot them one time. I shot them two times. I shot them three times. I shot them four times. I shot them five times. I shot them six times. I shot them seven times. I shot them eight times. I shot them nine times. I shot them ten times. I shot them multiple times. I saw all the male prison officers. I saw all the female prison officers. I saw them dropping. I saw them dropped. I saw them dropped on the ground. I saw them dropped on a prison ground. I saw them lying on the ground. I saw them lying on a prison ground. I saw them dying. I saw them bleeding. I saw their blood. I saw their blood on the ground. I saw their blood on a blood-filled ground. I saw their blood on a prison ground. I saw them dying. I saw them breathless. I saw them not breathing. I saw a static for a major. I saw them motionless. I saw them not shaking. I saw them not moving. I saw them dead. I saw them dead on the ground. I saw them dead on a prison ground. I saw them dead on a blood-filled ground. I walked. I walked forward. I walked past the dead prison officers. I walked farther. I opened all the prison gates. I opened all the cell doors. I freed all the prisoners. I freed all the Connecticut prisoners. I gave all the prisoners freedom. I gave freedom to all the prisoners. I spoke to all the prisoners. I told them to walk out. I told them to walk outside. I told them to walk outside the prison. I told them to wait outside. I told them to wait outside the prison. I told them to wait for me. I saw all the prisoners. I saw all the freed prisoners. I saw them walking. I saw them walking out. I saw them walking outside. I saw them outside. I saw them outside the prison. I saw them waiting. I saw them waiting outside. I saw them waiting outside the prison. I saw them waiting for me. I walked. I walked farther. I walked outside. I walked outside the prison. I walked forward. I walked past the prisoners. I stood in front of the prisoners. I looked farther. I rolled my eyes. I rolled my blue eyes. I saw something. I saw something strange. I saw something. I saw something strange happening. I saw hundreds of police motorbikes. I saw them appearing. I saw them appeared. I saw them appeared in front of me. I saw hundreds of police motorbikes. I saw them in front of me. I turned around. I faced the prisoners. I spoke to the prisoners. I told them to walk forward. I told them to walk towards the hundred motorbikes. I told them to jump on the motorbikes. I told them to ride on the motorbikes. I told them to ride faster. I told them to ride back home. I looked at the prisoners. I saw the freed prisoners. I saw them looking at me. I saw them speaking. I saw them speaking to me. I saw them thanking me. I saw them giving me thanks. I saw them giving me thanksgiving. I saw them thanking me for their freedom. I saw them thanking me for giving them freedom. I saw all the prisoners. I saw the freed prisoners. I saw them speaking. I saw them speaking to me. I saw them saying goodbye. I saw them saying goodbye to Peter Erickson. I saw them saying goodbye to the New York police officer. I saw them saying goodbye to me. I saw them walking. I saw them walking forward. I saw them walking past me. I saw them walking towards a hundred motorbikes. I saw them in front of police motorbikes. I saw them in front of a hundred motorbikes. I saw them jumping on the motorbikes. I saw them sitting on the police motorbikes. I saw them pushing their hands forward. I saw them grabbing the motorbikes. I saw them pushing their feet downwards. I saw them pushing harder. I saw them sparking. I saw them sparking the motorbikes. I saw them sparking one time. I saw them sparking two times. I saw them sparking three times. I saw them sparking multiple times. I saw them riding. I saw them riding on the motorbikes. I saw them riding with their head downwards. I saw them riding forward. I saw them riding faster. I saw them riding past me. I saw them riding faster. I saw them riding past Connecticut prison. I saw them riding faster. I saw them riding past Connecticut train stations. I saw them riding faster. I saw them riding past Connecticut police stations. I saw them riding faster. I saw them riding past police cars. I saw them riding faster. I saw them riding past police motorbikes. I saw them riding farther. I saw them riding back home. I walked. I walked forward. I walked past the prison. I walked past Connecticut prison. I walked towards my police motorbike. I stood in front of my police motorbike. I jumped. I jumped on my motorbike. I sat on my motorbike. I grabbed my giant gun. I pushed it. I pushed it inside my pocket. I pushed my hands forward. I grabbed my motorbike. I pushed my feet downwards. I pushed harder. I sparked my motorbike. I sparked it. I sparked it one time. I sparked it two times. I sparked it three times. I sparked it multiple times. I rode on my motorbike. I rode with my head downwards. I rode forward. I rode faster. I rode past the prison. I rode past Connecticut prison. I rode faster. I rode past Connecticut train stations. I rode faster. I rode past Connecticut police stations. I rode faster. I rode past police cars. I rode faster. I rode past police motorbikes. I rode faster. I rode past officers. I rode past walking officers. I rode faster. I rode past police officers. I rode past officers driving in police cars. I rode faster. I rode past officers riding on police motorbikes. I turned around. I looked backwards. I saw police cars. I saw police cars chasing me. I saw police motorbikes. I saw police motorbikes chasing me. I saw police officers. I saw them riding on police motorbikes. I saw them chasing me. I saw a police officer. I saw him riding on his police motorbike. I saw him riding faster. I saw him chasing me. I saw him pulling out a giant gun. I saw him pointing his gun. I saw him pointing the giant gun. I saw him pointing it at me. I saw him shooting. I saw him riding and shooting. I saw him shooting me. I saw him shooting me one time. I saw him shooting me two times. I saw him shooting me three times. I saw him shooting me multiple times. I saw nothing. I saw nothing happening. I saw nothing. I saw nothing happening to me. I pushed my hand inside my pocket. I pushed harder. I pulled out my machine gun. I grabbed my machine gun. I pointed it. I pointed it at the police officer. I shot the police officer. I shot him. I shot him one time. I shot him two times. I shot him three times. I shot him multiple times. I saw the police officer. I saw him dropping. I saw him dropped. I saw him dropped from his motorbike. I saw him dropped on the road. I saw him flying. I saw him flying farther. I saw him flying backwards. I saw his motorbike. I saw it rolling. I saw it rolling backwards. I saw it rolling farther. I saw the police officers. I saw them driving in police cars. I saw them driving faster. I saw them chasing me. I saw police officers. I saw them riding on police motorbikes. I saw them riding faster. I saw them chasing me. I saw the police officers. I saw them pulling out their guns. I saw them pulling out giant guns. I saw them pointing their guns. I saw them pointing giant guns. I saw them pointing guns at me. I saw them shooting. I saw them driving and shooting. I saw them riding and shooting. I saw them shooting me. I saw them shooting me one time. I saw them shooting two times. I saw them shooting three times. I saw them shooting four times. I saw them shooting five times. I saw them shooting six times. I saw them shooting seven times. I saw them shooting eight times. I saw them shooting nine times. I saw them shooting ten times. I saw them shooting multiple times. I saw nothing. I saw nothing happening. I saw nothing. I saw nothing happening to me. I pushed my hand inside my pocket. I grabbed my giant gun. I pointed my giant gun. I pointed my machine gun. I pointed my two giant guns. I pointed them at the police cars. I pointed them at the police motorbikes. I shot the police cars. I shot the police motorbikes. I shot them one time. I shot them two times. I shot them three times. I shot them four times. I shot them five times. I shot them six times. I shot them seven times. I shot them eight times. I shot them nine times. I shot them ten times. I shot them multiple times. I saw the police cars. I saw the police motorbikes. I saw them dropping. I saw them dropped. I saw them dropped on the road. I saw them rolling. I saw them rolling backwards. I saw them farther. I saw the police cars. I saw the police motorbikes. I saw them smashing. I saw them smashed. I saw them smashed on a road. I saw them blasting. I saw them blasted. I saw them busting. I saw them busted. I saw them bombing. I saw them bombed. I saw them burning. I saw them burned. I looked farther. I saw police officers. I saw them dropping. I saw them dropped. I saw them dropped from their motorbikes. I saw them rolling. I saw them rolling backwards. I looked farther. I saw them lying on a road. I saw them dying. I saw them dying on a road. I saw a static for a major. I saw them motionless. I saw them not shaking. I saw them not moving. I saw them dead. I saw them dead on a road. I turned. I looked forward. I pushed my hands inside my pockets. I pushed harder. I placed my giant gun. I placed my machine gun. I placed them inside my pockets. I pushed my hands forward. I grabbed my police motorbike. I rode on my police motorbike. I rode with my head downwards. I rode faster. I rode past the dead police officers. I rode faster. I rode past burning police cars. I rode past burned police cars. I rode faster. I rode past burning police motorbikes. I rode past burned police motorbikes. I rode faster. I rode past Connecticut police stations. I rode faster. I rode past Connecticut prisons. I rode faster. I rode past Connecticut train stations. I rode faster. I rode past police cars. I rode faster. I rode past police motorbikes. I rode faster. I rode past officers driving in police cars. I rode faster. I rode past officers riding on police motorbikes. I rode faster. I rode farther. I came across a state. I came across another state. I came across a West coast state.

11

THE ASSASSINATION MAN's JOURNEY

FROM CONNECTICUT TO WASHINGTON I rode on my police motorbike. I rode with my head downwards. I rode faster. I rode in a West coast state. I rode in Washington. I rode faster. I rode past Washington train stations. I rode faster. I rode past Washington police stations. I rode faster. I rode past police cars. I rode faster. I rode past police motorbikes. I rode faster. I rode past walking police officers. I rode faster. I rode past Washington police officers. I rode faster. I rode past officers driving in police cars. I rode faster. I rode past officers riding on police motorbikes. I rode farther. I came across a prison. I came across a prison in Washington. I came across a Washington prison. I parked my police motorbike. I parked it in front of the prison. I pushed my hand inside my pocket. I pulled out my giant gun. I grabbed my giant gun. I grabbed it. I jumped. I jumped off my police motorbike. I walked. I walked forward. I walked towards the prison. I stood in front of the prison. I stood in front of Washington prison. I stood in front of two giant gates. I looked at the two giant gates. I saw the two giant gates. I saw them locked. I rolled my eyes. I rolled my blue eyes. I saw something. I saw something strange. I saw something. I saw something strange happening. I looked at the two giant gates. I saw them opening. I saw them opening like a warrior. I saw them opening faster. I saw them opened. I walked. I walked inside the giant gates. I walked forward. I walked farther. I saw a male prison officer. I saw him farther. I saw him walking. I saw him walking forward. I saw him walking towards me. I saw him getting closer. I saw him getting closer to me. I saw him pulling a giant gun. I saw him grabbing a giant gun. I saw him pointing it at me. I saw him walking. I saw him walking and shooting. I saw him shooting. I saw him shooting me. I saw him shooting me one time. I saw him shooting me two times. I saw him shooting me three times. I saw him shooting me four times. I saw him shooting me five times. I saw him shooting me six times. I saw him shooting me seven times. I saw him shooting me eight times. I saw him shooting me nine times. I saw him shooting me ten times. I saw him shooting me multiple times. I saw nothing. I saw nothing happening. I saw nothing. I saw nothing happening to me. I saw the male prison officer. I saw him in front of me. I pushed my hand forward. I grabbed him. I grabbed his neck. I grabbed him with one hand. I raised him. I raised him with one hand. I raised him upwards. I raised him above the sky. I raised him above a prison sky. I was holding the prison officer. I was holding him with one hand. I looked at him. I smiled. I smiled at him. I rolled my eyes. I rolled my blue eyes. I threw the male prison officer. I threw him forward. I threw him farther. I saw the male prison officer. I saw him farther. I saw him flying. I saw him flying farther. I saw him flying. I saw him flying backwards. I saw him smashing. I saw him smashed. I saw him smashed on a wall. I saw him smashed on a heavenly wall. I saw him smashed on a prison wall. I saw him dropping. I saw him dropped. I saw him dropped on the ground. I saw him dropped on a prison ground. I looked farther. I saw the male prison officer. I saw him lying on the ground. I saw him lying on a prison ground. I saw him dying. I saw him bleeding. I saw his blood. I saw his blood on the ground. I saw his blood on a blood-filled ground. I saw his blood on a prison ground. I saw him dying. I saw him breathless. I saw him not breathing. I saw a static for a major. I saw him motionless. I saw him not shaking. I saw him not moving. I saw him dead. I saw him dead on the ground. I saw him dead on a blood-filled ground. I saw him dead on a prison ground. I walked. I walked forward. I walked towards the dead prison officer. I walked farther. I stood in front of the dead prison officer. I pushed my hands downwards. I pushed my hands inside his pockets. I searched him. I searched for the prison keys. I searched for the gate keys. I searched for the cell keys. I found the prison keys. I found the gate keys. I found the cell keys. I pulled out the prison keys. I pulled out the gate keys. I pulled out the cell keys. I grabbed the gate keys. I grabbed the cell keys. I walked. I walked forward. I walked past the dead prison officer. I walked farther. I looked farther. I saw a lot of prison officers. I saw a lot of male prison officers. I saw a lot of female prison officers. I saw them farther. I saw them running. I saw them running forward. I saw them running faster. I saw them running towards me. I saw them pulling out their guns. I saw them pulling out giant guns. I saw them grabbing giant guns. I saw them holding giant guns. I saw them pointing their guns. I saw them pointing giant guns. I saw them pointing guns at me. I saw them running. I saw them running and shooting. I saw them shooting. I saw them shooting me. I saw them shooting me one time. I saw them shooting me two times. I saw them shooting me three times. I saw them shooting me four times. I saw them shooting me five times. I saw them shooting me six times. I saw them shooting me seven times. I saw them shooting me eight times. I saw them shooting me nine times. I saw them shooting me ten times. I saw them shooting me multiple times. I saw nothing. I saw nothing happening. I saw nothing. I saw nothing happening to me. I grabbed my giant gun. I pointed it forward. I pointed it at the prison officers. I pointed it at the male prison officers. I pointed it at the female prison officers. I shot all the prison officers. I shot the male prison officers. I shot the female prison officers. I walked. I walked forward. I was walking. I was walking and shooting. I was shooting. I shot the male prison officers. I shot the female prison officers. I shot all of them. I shot them one time. I shot them two times. I shot them three times. I shot them four times. I shot them five times. I shot them six times. I shot them seven times. I shot them eight times. I shot them nine times. I shot them ten times. I shot them multiple times. I saw all the prison officers. I saw the male prison officers. I saw the female prison officers. I saw them dropping. I saw them dropped. I saw them dropped on the ground. I saw them dropped on a prison ground. I looked on the ground. I looked on a prison ground. I saw all the prison officers. I saw them lying on the ground. I saw them lying on a prison ground. I saw them dying. I saw them bleeding. I saw their blood. I saw their blood on the ground. I saw their blood on a blood-filled ground. I saw their blood on a prison ground. I saw them dying. I saw them breathless. I saw them not breathing. I saw a static for a major. I saw them motionless. I saw them not shaking. I saw them not moving. I saw them dead. I saw them dead on the ground. I saw them dead on a blood-filled ground. I saw them dead on a prison ground. I walked. I walked forward. I walked past the dead prison officers. I walked. I walked farther. I opened all the prison gates. I opened all the cell doors. I freed all the prisoners. I freed all the Washington prisoners. I gave all of the prisoners, freedom. I spoke to all the prisoners. I told them to walk out. I told them to walk outside. I told them to walk outside the prison. I told them to wait outside. I told them to wait outside the prison. I told them to wait for me. I saw all the Washington prisoners. I saw all the freed prisoners. I saw them walking. I saw them walking outside. I saw them outside. I saw them outside the prison. I saw them waiting. I saw them waiting outside. I saw them waiting outside the prison. I saw them waiting for me. I walked. I walked farther. I walked outside. I walked outside the prison. I walked forward. I walked past the prisoners. I stood in front of the prisoners. I looked. I looked forward. I looked at a road. I rolled my eyes. I rolled my blue eyes. I saw something. I saw something strange. I saw something. I saw something strange happening. I saw hundreds of police motorbikes. I saw them appearing. I saw them appeared. I saw them in front of me. I turned around. I faced all the prisoners. I spoke to all the prisoners. I told them to jump on the hundred motorbikes. I told them to ride on the motorbikes. I told them to ride faster. I told them to ride back home. I looked at all the prisoners. I saw the freed prisoners. I saw them looking at me. I saw them speaking. I saw them speaking to me. I saw them thanking Peter Erickson. I saw them thanking the New York police officer. I saw them thanking me. I saw them giving me thanks. I saw them giving me thanksgiving. I saw them thanking me for their freedom. I saw them thanking me for giving them freedom. I looked at all the prisoners. I saw them speaking. I saw them speaking to Peter Erickson. I saw them speaking to the New York police officer. I saw them speaking to me. I saw them saying goodbye. I saw them saying goodbye to Peter Erickson. I saw them saying goodbye to the New York police officer. I saw them saying goodbye to me. I saw them walking. I saw them walking forward. I saw them walking past me. I saw them walking towards the hundred motorbikes. I saw them in front of the police motorbikes. I saw them jumping on the motorbikes. I saw them sitting on the police motorbikes. I saw them pushing their hands forward. I saw them grabbing the motorbikes. I saw them pushing their feet downwards. I saw them pushing harder. I saw them sparking. I saw them sparking the police motorbikes. I saw them sparking one time. I saw them sparking two times.

I saw them sparking three times. I saw them sparking multiple times. I saw them riding. I saw them riding on the hundred motorbikes. I saw them riding with their heads downwards. I saw them riding forward. I saw them riding faster. I saw them riding past me. I saw them riding faster. I saw them riding past the prison. I saw them riding past Washington prison. I saw them riding faster. I saw them riding past Washington prisons. I saw them riding faster. I saw them riding past Washington police stations. I saw them riding faster. I saw them riding past police cars. I saw them riding faster. I saw them riding past police motorbikes. I saw them riding faster. I saw them riding past officers driving in police cars. I saw them riding faster. I saw them riding past officers riding on police motorbikes. I saw them riding faster. I saw them riding past Washington train stations. I saw them riding farther. I saw them riding back home. I walked. I walked forward. I walked towards my police motorbike. I jumped on my police motorbike. I sat on my police motorbike. I grabbed my giant gun. I pushed it inside my pocket. I pushed my hands forward. I grabbed my motorbike. I pushed my feet downwards. I pushed harder. I sparked my police motorbike. I sparked it one time. I sparked it two times. I sparked it three times. I sparked it multiple times. I rode on my police motorbike. I rode with my head downwards. I rode forward. I rode faster. I rode past the prison. I rode past Washington prison. I rode faster. I rode past Washington prisons. I rode faster. I rode past prisons in Washington. I rode faster. I rode past police stations. I rode faster. I rode past Washington police stations. I rode faster. I rode past police cars. I rode faster. I rode past police motorbikes. I rode faster. I turned. I turned around. I looked. I looked backwards. I saw police cars. I saw police motorbikes. I saw police officers driving in police cars. I saw police officers riding on police motorbikes. I saw driving police officers. I saw them driving in police cars. I saw them chasing me. I saw them getting closer. I saw them getting closer to me. I saw them outside their car windows. I saw them pulling out giant guns. I saw them pointing giant guns. I saw them pointing their guns at me. I saw them driving. I saw them driving and shooting. I saw them shooting me. I saw them shooting me one time. I saw them shooting me two times. I saw them shooting me three times. I saw them shooting me four times. I saw them shooting me five times. I saw them shooting me six times. I saw them shooting me seven times. I saw them shooting me eight times. I saw them shooting me nine times. I saw them shooting me ten times. I saw them shooting me multiple times. I saw nothing. I saw nothing happening. I saw nothing. I saw nothing happening to me. I pushed my hands inside my pockets. I pulled out my giant gun. I pulled out my machine gun. I grabbed my giant gun. I grabbed my machine gun. I pointed my giant gun. I pointed my machine gun. I pointed them at the police cars. I was riding on my police motorbike. I was riding and shooting. I shot the police cars. I shot them one time. I shot them two times. I shot them three times. I shot them four times. I shot them five times. I shot them six times. I shot them seven times. I shot them eight times. I shot them nine times. I shot them ten times. I shot them multiple times. I saw all the police cars. I saw them rolling. I saw them rolling backwards. I saw them rolling on the road. I saw the police cars. I saw the rolling cars. I saw them dropping. I saw them dropped. I saw them dropped on a road. I saw them blasting. I saw them blasted. I saw them busting. I saw them busted. I saw them bombing. I saw them bombed. I saw them on fire. I saw them burning. I saw them burned. I looked backwards. I saw police officers. I saw Washington police officers. I saw them riding. I saw them riding on police motorbikes. I saw them riding forward. I saw them riding faster. I saw them chasing me. I saw them getting closer. I saw them getting closer to me. I saw them pulling out giant guns. I saw them riding. I saw them riding on police motorbikes. I saw them riding on their motorbikes. I saw them getting closer. I saw them getting closer to me. I saw them riding faster. I saw them riding and shooting. I saw them shooting. I saw them shooting me. I saw them shooting me one time. I saw them shooting me two times. I saw them shooting me three times. I saw them shooting me four times. I saw them shooting me five times. I saw them shooting me six times. I saw them shooting me seven times. I saw them shooting me eight times. I saw them shooting me nine times. I saw them shooting me ten times. I saw them shooting me multiple times. I saw nothing. I saw nothing happening. I saw nothing. I saw nothing happening to me. I grabbed my machine gun. I pointed it. I pointed it at the police motorbikes. I was riding. I was riding and shooting. I shot the police officers. I shot the police motorbikes. I shot the police officers. I shot them one time. I shot them two times. I shot them three times. I shot them four times. I shot them five times. I shot them six times. I shot them seven times. I shot them eight times. I shot them nine times. I shot them ten times. I shot them multiple times. I saw the police officers. I saw them dropping. I saw them dropped. I saw them dropped on a road. I saw them dying. I saw them motionless. I saw them not shaking. I saw them not moving. I saw them dead. I saw them dead on a road. I saw the police motorbikes. I saw them rolling. I saw them rolling on a road. I saw them rolling backwards. I saw them dropping. I saw them dropped. I saw them dropped on a road. I saw them blasting. I saw them blasted. I saw them busting. I saw them busted. I saw them bombing. I saw them bombed. I saw them on fire. I saw them burning. I saw them burned. I turned. I turned around. I faced forward. I pushed my giant gun. I pushed it inside my pocket. I pushed my machine gun. I pushed it inside my pocket. I pushed my hands forward. I grabbed my police motorbikes. I pushed my feet downwards. I pushed harder. I rode on my police motorbike. I rode with my head downwards. I rode forward. I rode faster. I rode past the burning motorbikes. I rode faster. I rode past the burned motorbikes. I rode faster. I rode past the dead police officers. I rode faster. I rode past Washington police stations. I rode faster. I rode past Washington train stations. I rode faster. I rode past Washington police cars. I rode faster. I rode past Washington police motorbikes. I rode farther. I came across somewhere. I came across another state. I came across another West coast state.

12

THE ASSASSINATION MAN's JOURNEY

FROM WASHINGTON TO CALIFORNIA

I rode on my police motorbike. I rode faster. I rode inside Oregon. I rode faster. I rode past police stations. I rode faster. I rode past train stations. I rode farther. I rode inside Oregon prison. I shot all the prison officers. I grabbed the prison keys. I freed all the prisoners. I rode on my police motorbike. I rode faster. I rode inside another state. I rode inside another West coast state. I rode faster. I rode inside New Mexico. I rode faster. I rode past police stations. I rode faster. I rode past train stations. I rode farther. I rode inside New Mexico prison. I shot all the prison officers. I grabbed the prison keys. I freed all the prisoners. I rode on my police motorbike. I rode faster. I rode past police stations. I rode faster. I rode past train stations. I rode farther. I rode inside another state. I rode inside another West coast state. I rode inside Nevada. I rode faster. I rode past Nevada train stations. I rode faster. I rode past Nevada police stations. I rode farther. I rode inside Nevada prison. I shot all the prison officers. I grabbed the prison keys. I freed all the prisoners. I rode on my police motorbike. I rode faster. I rode past prisons. I rode faster. I rode past train stations. I rode faster. I rode past police stations. I rode farther. I rode inside another state. I rode inside another West coast state. I rode faster. I rode inside Montana. I rode faster. I rode past Montana train stations. I rode faster. I rode past Montana prisons. I rode faster. I rode past Montana police stations. I rode farther. I rode inside Montana prison. I shot all the prison officers. I grabbed the prison keys. I freed all the prisoners. I rode on my police motorbike. I rode with my head downwards. I rode faster. I rode past Montana prisons. I rode faster. I rode past Montana police stations. I rode faster. I rode past Montana train stations. I rode farther. I rode inside another state. I rode inside another West coast state. I rode faster. I rode inside Hawaii. I rode faster. I rode past Hawaii prisons. I rode faster. I rode past Hawaii train stations. I rode faster. I rode past Hawaii police stations. I rode farther. I rode inside Hawaii prison. I shot all the prison officers. I freed all the prisoners. I rode on my police motorbike. I rode faster. I rode past Hawaii prisons. I rode faster. I rode past Hawaii police stations. I rode faster. I rode past Hawaii train stations. I rode farther. I rode inside another state. I rode inside another West coast state. I rode faster. I rode inside Colorado. I rode faster. I rode past Colorado prisons. I rode faster. I rode past Colorado police stations. I rode faster. I rode past Colorado train stations. I rode farther. I rode inside Colorado prison. I shot all the prison officers. I grabbed the prison keys. I freed all the prisoners. I rode on my police motorbike. I rode faster. I rode past Colorado prisons. I rode faster. I rode past Colorado police stations. I rode faster. I rode past Colorado train stations. I rode farther. I rode inside another state. I rode inside another West coast state. I rode faster. I rode inside Arizona. I rode faster. I rode past Arizona train stations. I rode faster. I rode past Arizona police stations. I rode faster. I rode inside Arizona prisons. I rode faster. I rode inside Arizona prison. I shot all the prison officers. I grabbed the prison keys. I freed all the prisoners. I rode on my police motorbike. I rode faster. I rode past Arizona prisons. I rode faster. I rode past Arizona police stations. I rode faster. I rode past Arizona train stations. I rode farther. I rode inside another state. I rode inside another West coast state. I rode faster. I rode inside Alaska. I rode faster. I rode past Alaska train stations. I rode faster. I rode past Alaska prisons. I rode faster. I rode past Alaska police stations. I rode faster. I rode inside Alaska prison. I shot all the prison officers. I grabbed the prison keys. I freed all the prisoners. I rode on my police motorbike. I rode faster. I rode past Alaska prisons. I rode faster. I rode past Alaska police stations. I rode faster. I rode past Alaska train stations. I rode farther. I rode inside another state. I rode faster. I rode inside another West coast state. I rode faster. I rode inside California. I rode faster. I rode past California train stations. I rode faster. I rode past California police stations. I rode faster. I rode past California prisons. I rode faster. I rode inside a mansion. I rode inside a white mansion. I rode inside the mansion. I parked my motorbike. I parked it in front of the mansion. I grabbed my giant gun. I grabbed my machine gun. I jumped. I jumped off my motorbike. I walked. I walked inside the mansion. I walked farther. I saw a giant door. I walked. I walked towards the giant door. I stood in front of the giant door. I looked at the giant door. I saw the giant door. I saw it locked. I rolled my eyes. I rolled my blue eyes. I saw something. I saw something strange. I saw something. I saw something strange happening. I saw the giant door. I saw the locked door. I saw it opening. I saw it opening faster. I saw it opened. I walked. I walked inside it. I walked inside the room. I looked forward. I saw a white man. I saw him sitting on a chair. I saw him looking at me. I saw him speaking. I saw him speaking to me. I saw him asking for my name. I looked at him. I remembered him. I recognised him. I saw Snogun. I saw the assassinator. I saw Snogun. I saw the New York police officer. I saw my fellow police officer. I saw the man who assassinated Peter Erickson. I saw the man who assassinated the New York police officer. I saw the man who assassinated me. I grabbed two giant guns. I grabbed my machine gun. I grabbed my giant gun. I pointed it. I pointed it forward. I pointed it at Snogun. I shot Snogun. I shot him. I shot him one time. I shot him two times. I shot him three times. I shot him four times. I shot him five times. I shot him six times. I shot him seven times. I shot him eight times. I shot him nine times. I shot him ten times. I shot him multiple times. I saw Snogun. I saw the assassination man. I saw nothing. I saw nothing happening. I saw nothing. I saw nothing happening to him. I saw Snogun. I saw him jumping. I saw him jumping off his chair. I saw him jumping above the sky. I saw him landing. I saw him landing on the ground. I saw him landing on a mansion ground. I saw him landing on a white ground. I saw Snogun. I saw the assassinator. I saw him standing. I saw him standing in front of me. I saw him looking at me. I saw him pushing his hand forward. I saw him grabbing me. I saw him grabbing me with one hand. I saw him grabbing my neck. I saw him grabbing my neck with one hand. I saw him raising me. I saw him raising me upwards. I saw him raising me above the sky. I saw him holding me. I saw him holding me with one hand. I saw him holding me above the sky. I saw Snogun. I saw the assassinator. I saw him looking at me. I saw him smiling. I saw him smiling at me. I saw him rolling his eyes. I saw him rolling his green eyes. I saw him throwing me. I saw him throwing me forward. I saw him throwing me farther. I smashed on the giant door. I dropped. I dropped on the ground. I saw Snogun. I saw him walking. I saw him walking forward. I saw him walking towards me. I saw him in front of me. I saw him looking at me. I saw him smiling. I saw him smiling at me. I saw Snogun. I saw him pushing his hand downwards. I saw him grabbing me. I saw him grabbing me with one hand. I saw him holding me. I saw him holding me with one hand. I saw him holding me above the sky. I saw him looking at me. I saw him smiling. I saw him smiling at me. I saw him rolling his eyes. I saw him rolling his green eyes. I saw him throwing me. I saw him throwing me forward. I saw him throwing me farther. I smashed. I smashed against a wall. I smashed against a white wall. I smashed against a mansion wall. I dropped. I dropped downwards. I was weakened. I felt heavy pain. I suffered in heavy pain. I was breathless. I was not breathing. I was motionless. I was not shaking. I was not moving. I saw Snogun. I saw the assassinator. I saw him in front of me. I saw him looking at me. I saw him smiling. I saw him smiling at me. I saw him walking. I saw him walking forward. I saw him walking towards me. I saw him pushing his hand downwards. I saw him grabbing me. I saw him grabbing me with one hand. I saw him holding me. I saw him holding me with one hand. I saw him holding me above the sky. I saw him holding me above the mansion sky. I saw him looking at me. I saw him smiling. I saw him smiling at me. I saw him rolling his eyes. I saw him rolling his green eyes. I saw him throwing me. I saw him throwing me forward. I saw him throwing me farther. I smashed. I smashed on a wall. I smashed on a heavenly wall. I smashed on a white wall. I dropped. I dropped on the ground. I dropped on a white ground. I dropped on a mansion ground. I was weakened. I suffered in weakness. I felt weakened. I felt heavy pain. I was breathless. I was not breathing. I was motionless. I was not shaking. I was not moving. I was dying. I was bleeding. I saw my blood. I saw my blood on the ground. I saw my blood on a white ground. I saw my blood on a mansion ground. I remembered. I remembered my name. I remembered who I was. I remembered I was Peter Erickson. I remembered I was the New York police officer. I remembered I was not human. I remembered I was a machine. I remembered I was a robot. I remembered I was a human robot. I looked on the ground. I looked on my left hand side. I saw something. I saw my machine gun. I grabbed my machine gun. I jumped. I jumped upwards. I stood upwards. I stood in front of Snogun. I grabbed my machine gun. I pointed it forward. I pointed it at Snogun. I shot Snogun. I shot him. I shot him one time. I shot him two times. I shot him three times. I shot him four times. I shot him five times. I shot him six times. I shot him seven times. I shot him eight times. I shot him nine times. I shot him ten times. I shot him multiple times. I saw Snogun. I saw him dropping. I saw him dropped. I saw him dropped on the ground. I saw him lying on the ground. I saw him lying on a white ground. I saw him lying on a mansion ground. I saw him dying. I saw weakened. I saw him in weakness. I saw him suffering. I saw him in pain. I saw him in heavy pain. I saw a static for a major. I saw him breathless. I saw him not breathing. I saw him motionless. I saw him not shaking. I saw him not moving. I saw Snogun. I saw the assassinator. I saw the assassination man. I saw the man who assassinated Peter Erickson. I saw the man who assassinated the New York police officer. I saw the man who assassinated me. I saw Snogun. I saw the New York police officer. I saw my fellow police officer. I saw him dead. I saw him dead on the ground. I saw him dead on a white ground. I saw him dead on a mansion ground. I walked. I walked forward. I saw a table. I saw a brown table. I walked towards the brown table. I looked on top of the table. I saw a book. I saw my book. I saw the book of justice. I saw my book. I saw the book I wrote years ago. I saw the book of justice. I saw it on the brown table. I grabbed my book. I grabbed the book of justice. I placed it inside my pockets. I grabbed my machine gun. I placed it inside my pocket. I pushed my hands downwards. I grabbed Snogun. I grabbed the dead man. I placed him on top of my shoulder. I carried Snogun. I carried him on my shoulder. I opened the giant door. I carried Snogun. I carried him outside. I carried him outside the mansion. I walked. I walked farther. I walked outside. I walked outside the governor's mansion. I walked forward. I walked towards my police motorbike. I stood in front of my police motorbike. I grabbed Snogun. I placed him at the back of my motorbike. I jumped on my police motorbike. I rode faster. I rode outside. I rode outside the mansion. I rode outside the governor's mansion. I rode faster. I rode past California police stations. I rode faster. I rode past California train stations. I rode faster. I rode past California prisons. I rode faster. I rode inside a California prison. I shot all the prison officers. I grabbed the prison keys. I freed all the prisoners. I rode on my police motorbike. I rode with my head downwards. I rode faster. I rode past California prisons. I rode faster. I rode past California police stations. I rode faster. I rode past California train stations. I rode farther. I rode inside another state. I rode inside Texas. I rode faster. I rode past Texas train stations. I rode faster. I rode past Texas police stations. I rode faster. I rode past Texas prisons. I rode farther. I rode faster. I rode inside a prison. I parked my police motorbike. I parked it in front of the prison. I grabbed my machine gun. I jumped. I jumped off my police motorbike. I grabbed Snogun. I placed him on my shoulder. I walked. I walked forward. I walked towards the prison. I saw the prison gate. I saw two giant gates. I saw them locked. I looked at the giant gate. I rolled my eyes. I rolled my blue eyes. I saw something. I saw something strange. I saw something. I saw something strange happening. I saw the two giant gates. I saw the locked gates. I saw them opening. I saw them opening faster. I saw them opened. I walked. I walked inside the prison. I walked forward. I saw a reception. I saw one prison officer. I saw a male prison officer. I saw him sitting on a black chair. I saw him sitting in the reception. I walked. I walked forward. I walked towards the male prison officer. I stood in front of him. I spoke to him. I told him a story. I told him my story. I explained something. I explained something to him. I told him I was not a human. I told him I was a machine. I told him I was a human robot. I saw the male prison officer. I saw him looking at my shoulder. I saw him looking at Snogun. I saw him looking at a dead man. I saw the male prison officer. I saw him asking me a question. I saw him asking me about Snogun. I saw him asking me about the dead man. I looked at the male prison officer. I spoke to him. I told him a story. I told him my story. I told him I wrote the book of justice. I told him I wanted to put an end to the death penalty and change the American justice system. I told him I set off a journey to the governor's mansion. I told him I was followed. I told him I was followed by Snogun. I told him I was shot and murdered. I told him I was shot and murdered by my fellow police officer. I told him I was shot and murdered by Snogun. I told him Snogun grabbed the book of justice. I told him Snogun rode towards the governor's mansion. I told him Snogun shot and killed the governor. I told him Snogun murdered the California governor. I told him Snogun became the new governor in California. I spoke to the Texas male prison officer. I told him another story. I told him a story about Black Arnold. I told him a story about a black man. I told him a story about the prisoner. I told him a story about a black prisoner. I told him a story about a prisoner in Texas. I told him a story about a death row prisoner. I told him a story about the innocent prisoner. I told him a story about an innocent man. I told him a story about Black Arnold. I told him Black Arnold is an innocent man. I told him Black Arnold was riding on his motorbike. I told him Black Arnold was riding home. I told him Black Arnold saw me dead. I told him Black Arnold saw me dead on a road. I told him black Arnold jumped off his motorbike. I told him Black Arnold tried to help me. I told him Black Arnold was extremely helpful. I told him Snogun called the police. I told him the police arrived. I told him the police arrived and saw Black Arnold in front of my dead body. I told him the police suspected Black Arnold. I told him the police suspected him as the murderer. I told him the police arrested Black Arnold. I told him the police sentenced Black Arnold to death. I told him the police gave Black Arnold a death penalty. I told him Black Arnold is an innocent man. I told him to free Black Arnold. I looked at the male prison officer. I saw tears. I saw tears running down his eyes. I saw the male prison officer. I saw him. I saw him crying. I saw him in tears. I saw him in heavy tears. I saw him looking at me. I saw him crying. I saw him speaking. I saw him speaking to me. I saw him telling me about an execution. I saw him telling me about Black Arnold execution date. I saw him telling me that Black Arnold will be executed tonight. I saw the male prison officer. I saw him grabbing a telephone. I saw him ringing. I saw him ringing the execution chamber. I saw him talking. I saw him talking to Jackson. I saw him talking to the executioner. I saw him saying something. I saw him saying something to another prison officer. I saw the executioner. I saw him stopping the execution. I saw him stopping the execution of Black Arnold. I saw the prison officers. I saw them grabbing Black Arnold. I saw them walking. I saw them walking with Black Arnold. I saw them taking Black Arnold. I saw them taking him outside. I saw them taking him to Peter Erickson. I saw Black Arnold. I saw him outside. I saw him outside Texas death row. I saw him outside Texas prison. I saw Black Arnold. I saw the innocent man. I saw the freed man. I saw the freed prisoner. I saw him in front of Peter Erickson. I saw him in front of a New York police officer. I saw him in front of me. I saw him looking at me. I saw him speaking. I saw him speaking to me. I saw him thanking Peter Erickson. I saw him thanking the New York police officer. I saw him thanking his hero. I saw him giving me thanks. I saw him giving me thanksgiving. I saw him thanking me. I walked. I walked forward. I walked towards my police motorbike. I jumped on my motorbike. I spoke to Black Arnold. I told him to jump on my motorbike. I saw Black Arnold. I saw him walking. I saw him walking forward. I saw him walking towards my motorbike. I saw him in front of my motorbike. I saw him jumping on my motorbike. I saw him sitting on my motorbike. I saw him sitting at the back of my motorbike. I grabbed my machine gun. I pushed it inside my pockets. I pushed my hands forward. I grabbed my police motorbike. I pushed my feet downwards. I pushed harder. I sparked my motorbike. I sparked it one time. I sparked it two times. I sparked it three times. I sparked it multiple times. I rode on my motorbike. I rode with Black Arnold. I rode with a black man. I rode with a Black Death row prisoner. I rode with an innocent man. I rode with a freed prisoner. I rode with a freed man. I rode faster. I rode past Texas prison. I rode faster. I rode past prisons. I rode faster. I rode past Texas prisons. I rode faster. I rode past police stations. I rode faster. I rode past Texas police stations. I rode faster. I rode past train stations. I rode farther. I rode past all the West coast state. I rode farther. I rode past a lot of East coast states. I rode farther. I rode back to New York. I rode back home. I am Peter Erickson. I am a New York police officer. I am the man who wrote the book of justice. I am the man who wanted to put an end to the death penalty. I am the man who wanted to change the American justice system. I am the man who saved the life of Black Arnold. I am the man who saved the life of a death row prisoner. I am the man who saved the life of a Black Death row prisoner. I am the man who saved the life of an innocent man. I am the man who wrote the book of justice. I will put an end to the death penalty one day. I will change the American justice system one day. I am Peter Erickson. I am a New York police officer. This is my journey to save Black Arnold. This is my journey to save the life of a black man. This is my journey to save the life of an innocent man. This is my journey to save the life of a black prisoner. This is my journey to save the life of an innocent prisoner. This is my journey to end the death penalty. This is my journey to change the American justice system.